I0727396

STRANGE SHORTS

(A COLLECTION OF SHORT STORIES FOR TEENAGERS AND PERENNIAL TEENAGERS)

Lesley Ann Eden

MAPLE
PUBLISHERS

STRANGE SHORTS

Author: Lesley Ann Eden

Copyright © Lesley Ann Eden (2025)

The right of Lesley Ann Eden to be identified as author of this work has been asserted by the author in accordance with section 77 and 78 of the Copyright, Designs and Patents Act 1988.

First Published in 2025

ISBN 978-1-83538-652-1 (Paperback)
        978-1-83538-653-8 (Hardback)

Cover design adapted from a painting by S.J.Jameson. Witches Stitch.

Book layout by:
        White Magic Studios
        www.whitemagicstudios.co.uk

Published by:
        Maple Publishers
        Fairbourne Drive, Atterbury,
        Milton Keynes,
        MK10 9RG, UK
        www.maplepublishers.com

A CIP catalogue record for this title is available from the British Library.

All rights reserved. No part of this book may be reproduced or translated by any form or by any means, electronic or mechanical, including photocopying, recording or by any information storage and retrieval system without written permission from the author.

The views expressed in this work are solely those of the author and do not necessarily reflect the views of the publisher, and the publisher hereby disclaims any responsibility for them.

For LIBBY ...all is possible my darling girl!

CONTENTS

AUTHOR'S NOTE

Dear Reader,

I hope you enjoy this collection of short stories as many of them are based on my own real experiences, having had strange happenings occur all my life and in relaying them to you, I hope your imagination will be stirred to peep through a crack in the Universe to worlds beyond the beyond, where you may glimpse yourself in your true form and discover your life's purpose. For when you encounter the 'strangeness' of things you will come to know that all is not what it seems, so never give up on your dreams; for all is possible. Dream big and imagine you have created the very best for yourself- remember-'as above, so below'. Just believe in yourself.

Most of all, love yourself and you will love others as they will love you.

'Love is all you need!'(John Lennon)

I wish you 'Love'

Lesley Ann Eden

THE BOY NEXT DOOR

The first time I saw him he was sitting dejectedly on his front door step. I was moving into a flat next door and couldn't help but notice him staring miserably into space as I raced in and out, juggling cases and congeries of boxes piled high with my belongings. He was a gangly, pallid youth, sitting crouched with his long legs heaved up under his chin and his straggly arms dangling aimlessly over his knees. It was a Saturday evening and as a teacher of boys of his age, I thought it odd that he wasn't out with his mates. His lonely, sad demeanour echoed a thousand torments of the struggling teenager coming to terms with both physical and mental changes of the 'neither child, nor adult' syndrome. His gloomy, sunken eyes glazed in a far-away expression did not register my brief smile as I passed his gate with my last box of books.

The next few days during half term were spent unpacking and organizing my new apartment into a cosy cocoon- a place to escape the classroom war zone and whilst emptying a delicate box of china in the kitchen, I noticed for the first time the extensive garden next door. I didn't have much time to tidy my own small, concrete plot speckled with a few old planters full of dead weeds and hadn't noticed the large orchard next door where they had erected a lovely swing for their children. I suddenly remembered the forlorn teenage boy who was sitting on the steps the evening I moved in and momentarily, I thought I saw him walking in the shade of the apple trees. I hadn't seen him since that first evening and I wondered which school he attended. It certainly wasn't mine as I would have known him.

Carefully placing a beautiful, floral milk jug, which had belonged to my grandmother, on a display shelf next to the window, I was distracted by strange movement shimmering like a watery mirage in the sunlight, flickering through the apple trees. It wasn't the wind shaking the branches, but a hidden force pulsing through the air which disappeared when I blinked. I thought I must have imagined the vision and returned to my unpacking when the boy's pasty face peered from behind a Hawthorn bush. I thought he must be playing hide and seek with a sibling, as he was secretly peeping. Sure enough a little girl of about seven years of age ran towards the swing. She was dressed in a sweet pink coat and her long brown ringlets danced over her shoulders as she ran. She climbed into the swing seat, shuffling her bottom along the wooden plank and began pushing her legs into the air to gain momentum and then from nowhere the boy, her brother, sprang into action pushing her higher and higher skywards. She screamed with laughter and then after a few moments delight, ran off leaving the boy staring into space. It was a strange moment as there was no interaction between them, except for the movement of the swing and no recognition of each other. Momentarily, I turned on the tap to wash a dusty cup and when I looked up the boy had disappeared.

Term began and I was busy marking essays in the evening and rising early to take the bus to school so I didn't see the boy again until one morning -it was a Friday I recall, as I was looking forward to the weekend and the sun was rising, streaking the sky with orange flashes, washing the trees with a glowing pink aura and there he was gliding through the bushes, almost as if his feet were off the ground. I stared through the bathroom window wondering what he was doing so early in the morning wandering in the garden. He wasn't wearing a school uniform but dressed in brown trousers and black hoodie. He appeared sickly and weak. I thought he must be off school with a bug. I wanted to stay to watch him but I had a bus to catch and was running late, so I abandoned my watch post.

Later that day, after school it was lovely to relax with a glass of wine in my small backyard which I had transformed with potted plants, small ferns and hanging baskets of trailing geraniums and I was just closing my eyes when a peal of girlish laughter rang across from behind the wall. I got up to nosily peer over the fence and saw the little girl playing with her dolls and an imaginary friend as she poured them pretend tea from a little plastic tea pot. The game was delightful to watch except that the longer I looked, the more I became intrigued by the invisible, imaginary friend who seemed to be communicating with the little girl in a very plausible manner. She constantly chatted away like a little happy canary. Listening and watching the enchanting scene, my Mother's words flooded back:

"Well, in the end I had to take you to the Doctor because you would spend hours on end talking to invisible people. I mean it wasn't like any other normal child just pretending to have an imaginary friend. Oh no! You were really talking to …whoever? Then you would put things they gave you into a little basket, imaginary things and it would go on and on. I don't know who you were talking to but they told you strange things; it wasn't normal. The Doctor said you had an over-imaginative mind and that you would grow out of it! The sedative to make you sleep didn't work either! All that talk of a strange lady in your room was nonsense until we found you with the bed sheets tied around your neck strangling you! Well that was unbelievable as you couldn't have done it yourself, so we had everything in your room burnt!"

I was born with a psychic gift, which my Mother, being a staunch Catholic, continually tried to shatter and make me admit that all I saw, heard and felt from beyond was a sin. It wasn't until her death that she accepted my psionic skills and asked me in her dying breath if I could still see forwards like I used to? When I asked her why she wanted to know, she replied: "because I could do the same!"

Her words echoed from the past then faded as I continued to spy on the scene and when the little girl was called in for her tea the wind ruffled the table cloth and rattled the tea cups as though an invisible energy was still seated at the table. My phone rang interrupting the picture and I went indoors to answer it leaving behind the strange encounter.

That night before I went to bed I spent a little time in my backyard gazing at the stars pondering my unusual interest in the children next door. It was the boy who enticed my curiosity more than anything, as he seemed so alone, desolate and bereft of friends, which for a teenager of his age was odd. I swear I didn't mean to, but I suddenly found myself spying over the garden fence. Through the French windows I saw the family –Mother, Father, and little daughter sitting together on the couch watching a quiz game on the television. They were totally absorbed by the programme and occasionally shouted out answers or laughed spontaneously. Outside sitting on the step, with his face pinned against the window was the boy. It was shocking to see him almost pining to be inside with his family, like a lost puppy left outside in the dark. I was hesitant to do anything but impulsively I climbed over the fence further down the path as it was not so high and crept towards where he was sitting. I was so close that I could almost touch his hair but as I reached out to him he disappeared and I was left in full view of the family, standing stupidly waving. I was so embarrassed as we had never met before, so I pretended to wave at them to attract their attention. The Father got up immediately to investigate the strange intruder. I introduced myself explaining that my kitten was missing and I was looking for her and as I had just moved in next door she might have wandered over to their house. The family were very kind about the whole affair and I hurriedly left through their back gate not wanting to cause any further disruption. I knew I had seen the boy and his disappearance only compounded my concern for him. I went to bed thoroughly confused by the incident and ashamed to be caught wandering in my neighbour's garden without permission and I wondered if I should buy a kitten to give me an alibi for my strange behaviour?

During the next few days I avoided the neighbours and spying on their children in the garden. I buried myself in my work, but coming home late one evening I saw him again forlornly sitting on his front doorstep like the day I moved in. I waved to him but his attention was elsewhere and I thought it best to leave him alone. The next morning, being Saturday, I took a lazy breakfast out on my patio and was enjoying my first cup of coffee when a delightful little voice spoke from over the fence. She was spying on me! She had placed her little chair right up to the fence giving her a bird's eye view of my compact garden.

"Hello," I greeted her with my best sweet, infant friendly charm and she smiled.

"Where's your kitten?" she asked, almost accusingly. I suddenly felt guilty and choked on my sip of coffee, which made her giggle and my lie more obvious.

"Er, she's indoors!" I replied unconvincingly, trying to cover up my embarrassment.

"Can I see her? What's her name? Mine's Matty." She quickly blurted out.

But I was saved by her Mother who popped her head over the fence and apologised for Matty's intrusion. She also asked about the kitten and I said I was keeping her indoors for a while. I could tell by Matty's expression that she didn't believe me for one minute!

"Please, if you are free this afternoon have tea with us in the garden? I believe it's going to be a nice day and you can meet some other neighbours."

I graciously accepted her invitation and noted Matty's disdainful expression as she was made to climb down from her chair, spoiling her fun.

Later that afternoon I appeared bearing gifts of chocolates and flowers by way of an apology for my night-prowling incident and was introduced to a few other neighbours. I noticed a lovely photo of the adolescent boy, their son, on the mantelpiece. When I had seen him previously he looked unwell and forlorn, so it was lovely to see him relaxed and smiling in the photo. As I stood by the fireplace looking at the photo, a neighbour introduced herself and whispered-"what a tragedy?"

I looked puzzled and she continued, "Oh I'm sorry, you're new to the neighbourhood, you don't know of course?"

I shook my head and asked her to explain. She cautiously took me to one side and said, "That was young Timmy. Please don't mention him. The family are still in mourning. He ran out in front of a car a few months ago to save their little puppy and both he and the dog were killed instantly." She moved away quietly to join the others in the garden while I stayed, staring in shock at the winsome smile of the teenage boy.

"You see him don't you?" whispered Matty standing by my side gazing up at me. I didn't reply. "You do, I know you do. You are like me- we see things don't we? I know you don't have a kitten!" she whispered sweetly. "Come and see the swing?" she urged tugging my hand and I let her lead me into the garden under the apple trees where the swing was gently swaying in the hot, windless afternoon.

THE BOY AND THE BLACK SWAN

Inside an ancient fourteenth century church a film crew are preparing to record an interview for their programme 'Strange Tales'.

Director: Is the old timer ready Sam?

Interviewer: Yes, all ready.

Director: Are we clear to roll?

Interviewer: Yes, all clear.

Director: Rolling...Action!

Clapperboard girl: Strange Tales, interviewing Daniel Creedy, Take one!

Interviewer: Well Mr. Creedy, we are here in this amazing fourteenth century church for you to tell us about your special strange story.

Dan: Well son what would you like to know?

Director: CUT! Look Mr. Creedy you are speaking to many people remember? Please don't address the interviewer directly or call him son.

Dan: No Sir, that's fine sir!

Director: Or call him or me Sir!

Dan : Yes Sir, I mean no Sir!

The Director throws his hands up in the air and motions the crew to begin again. Clapperboard girl goes through the ritual again.

Interviewer: Let's start with you Mr. Creedy tell us a little about yourself, I mean your Father was in the American Airforce and came here and married a young girl from this village. Is that correct?

Dan: Yes Sir, that's correct Sir, I mean young man!

Director: CUT! I tell you what Sam, let's just let him say what he wants and cue him in now and then. Ready to roll...Action!

Clapperboard girl: Strange Tales, interviewing Daniel Creedy, Take three!

Interviewer: So your Father and Mother got married here in this very church and later you were baptised here. Is that true?

Dan: Very true, very true.

Interviewer: So you grew up here and I understand that you spent your childhood travelling back and forth between here and Louisiana in America?

Dan: Also true! I guess that's why I speak the way I do! (He laughs) I aint got no fancy English accent!

Interviewer: You have a very strange, interesting story Mr. Creedy which evolves around this church would you like to tell us how it all started?

Dan: Well I guess I was around twelve years old an' just started at the big school an' we was preparin' to go on a school camping trip so we had ta practice puttin' up our one man tent an spendin' the night outside.

Interviewer: Oh I bet that was fun?

Dan: Well, no it weren't because I didn't like camping, not one little bit, especially after what happened!

Interviewer: What happened?

Dan: Well, I think there was four of us, yeas four boys puttin' up our tents by the river an' preparing to spend the night trying out our tents and equipment.

Interviewer: That sounds exciting...

Dan: Well, no it wasn't 'cos I already told ya I didn't like camping, it weren't no fun ta me!

Interviewer: Sorry, please continue.

Dan: We got our tents made ready an I was asleep in my sleeping bag with a blanket covering my head when I felt something shuffling up the blanket from outside. I switched on my torch an' there was a darn black swan with its long black neck, orange beak and beady black eyes staring at me! Well I hollowed, an' I screeched, an' made a hullabaloo like ya never heard afore! All the other boys come runnin' an' I am inside the tent scramblin' ta get out an the boys outside are scrambling ta get in and the whole damn tent collapses. Well, I kinda faint at the shock of it all.

Interviewer: A black swan? How on earth did it get in your tent?

Dan: If I knew that I wouldna be tellin' the story, now would I?

Interviewer: So the boys managed to get you out of the tent but where did the swan go?

Dan: If I knew that it wouldna be a mystery, now would it?

Interviewer: So what happened next?

Dan: Well the boys helped me to recover from the shock an' I refused to go back in the tent, so I packed up all my things and began to walk home. I wasn't havin' no more black swan trying to attack me in the middle of the night! I walked up through the village and got to the railway bridge just as the sun was risin'. I looked down and there was a little boy about six years old starin' up at me. He was only wearin' a long cotton nightgown that came down to his feet and brown slippers. Well I asks him what he doin' there, an he says he's lost an' I asks about his Ma and Pa but he don't know. So I figured that my Ma would know what to do and find the little fella's parents.

Interviewer: Did he give his name?

Dan: He didn't seem to know that either an' I thought the poor little fella might have hit his head or somethin' to make him forget a thing like that!

Interviewer: What did your Mother say?
Dan: Well she was as perplexed as me and Pa was away workin' so she made him a bed next to mine thinkin' that come the mornin' we would get help. The little fella settled down in bed an' I went to sleep listenin' to the radio, I mean I was still in shock and needed the comfort of voices around me.

Interviewer: What happened in the morning?

Dan: Hold on there a minute, I aint done yet!

Interviewer: Sorry, please continue.

Dan: Like I said, I went to sleep with the radio on but woke up a short while later and was darn shocked to see what I saw! (He pauses and takes a deep breath while the interviewer is eager to learn what transpired but doesn't interrupt.) Well without a word of a lie, the boy was sitting on the edge of the bed and the black swan with its big wings splayed out wide, sat beside him. I calls out to him, "what's that damn thing doin' in here?" And he says it flew in through the window but the windows were closed and not big enough for the damn thing to fly in. So I shouts for Ma an she comes runnin' in as as fast as a coyote chasin' a rabbit. But when she opens the door, the swan disappeared and the boy was layin' there asleep all innocent like a lamb. Well Ma thinks I'm goin' crazy talkin' bout the swan an all, an she thinks I'm kinda sick.

Interviewer: Oh you mean crazy?

Dan: Call it what you will, but I knows what I saw! In the mornin' the boy was gone. Well I was kinda relieved by that because I thought he was up to no good.

Interviewer: Did you see him again?

Dan: Sure did! It was a few days later when I walked down to this here church an' saw the boy standin' by the old graves. Well, I'm tellin' ya, I saw as clear as day, the little fella turns into the black swan. It rises on its webbed feet and then flies away.

Interviewer: My goodness that must have been a shock?

Dan: Indeed it was!

Interviewer: Now just for a moment we have some historical facts and some local myths concerning this story. Dr. Trevor Eastwood is an expert on local history, please tell us what you know which might shed a little light on this mystery.

Dr. Trevor Eastwood: Well those of you who know this area, will appreciate that before King John was crowned King of England his father King Henry II gave him the local castle to keep him away from court, where he was known to be a bit of a trouble maker. In fact when Prince John did become King he was either thought of as a tyrant or a reformer. He certainly wasn't one of our most popular Kings that's for sure. However in his lustful youth he was said to have sired a few bastard children around these parts and the symbol for a bastard child of royalty is the black swan.

Interviewer: How interesting, in fact the local pub is called the Black Swan, I understand?

Dr.Trevor Eastwood: It is and the image of the Black Swan is sometimes denoted by a golden crown on its head, symbolising that the bastard child was fathered by a King.

Interviewer: Very intriguing and thank you Dr. Eastwood. Now let us hear from Mrs. Tockwith, a collector of local myths and legends. Mrs. Tockwith what can you tell us about this story?

Mrs. Tockwith: Well, Mr. Eastwood is quite right about King John and before he was crowned King he was known around here as a wild, rowdy, riotous young man who took whatever he wanted, when he wanted and that included all the pretty young girls.

Interviewer: Really? Well that seems to fit the bad King John image.

Mrs. Tockwith: Precisely! Well as legend has it, there were two sisters Granny Blythe and Granny Goodwill who were both 'soothsayers' healers, midwives or as some called them 'witches'. They both had beautiful Granddaughters Aramith and Tabatha and any maiden associated with Prince John was well-rewarded for their services, especially if they became pregnant and were paid to keep silent. There was great rivalry between the two young girls to gain Prince John's attention and it was Granny Blythe's Granddaughter Aramith, who actually became the Prince's favourite, which angered Granny Goodwill and Tabatha. Together they threatened to cast a spell on Aramith if she became pregnant with Prince John's son and curse him for all eternity.

Interviewer: I see, and what was the curse?

Mrs.Tockwith: It is said that if Aramith was to bear a son, they would turn the child into a black swan so that all would know that he was a royal bastard.

Interviewer: But the boy child is sometimes seen with the black swan...

Dan: Well I sure as hell seen him and seen him turn into the swan, I'm tellin' ya it's the truth, it's the whole damn truth!

Dan becomes agitated and moves out of his chair as a nurse quickly moves forwards to take him off the set.

The director whispers to keep him contained as they are about to wrap up the interview. Dan is escorted to the pews at the back of the church.

Interviewer: Yes, thank you Dan, we hear your story. Mrs. Tockwith can you explain this phenomenon?

Mrs. Tockwith: I can only say what is contained in the legend as I am not an expert on such things, but when a spell like that is cast, the instigator has a duty to allow the victim an allotted amount of time in his own body before turning into the animal and the animal is allowed a separate space in which to be itself before taking over the body of the victim. This is universal law and that is why sometimes the boy is the swan and on other occasions they are separate beings.

Interviewer: Well that certainly explains things Mrs. Tockwith and thank you for your time. We have one more surprise to reveal and that is our researcher has unveiled the interesting fact that Dan's Mother was distantly related to Aramith. Isn't that amazing and may be the reason for Dan having a connection with the story? Thank you Mr. Eastwood for your information and filling us in with some historical details. Thank you everyone for watching another amazing strange tale. See you next week.

Director: Quiet in the studio! (Everyone pauses) It's a wrap!

The crew begin to pack away equipment and tidy up the church. Sam, the interviewer walks over to Dan who has been sedated by the nurse and is smiling.

Sam: Thank you Dan for your input. Sorry you have to go back to the hospital now, I would have loved to talk with you further.

Dan nods his head while he is helped into a wheelchair.

Sam: Can I just ask you one more thing Dan?

Dan nods in agreement.

Sam: Do you still see the boy and the black swan?

Dan grins and whispers-"I sure do, why they're here now! See…" Dan holds out a black feather with a little white tip as another black feather gently floats down from nowhere and lands on Sam's foot.

MOUNTAIN MONSTER

Do you know what it's like to have to keep proving yourself to others? I mean, they don't bully me, well not like they used to, but I suppose I want them to be nice to me; I want them to accept me. We're in this together and the Mountaineering Club is open to everyone and I can't help it if I'm the youngest! I mean my parents paid for the trip as well as theirs and here in Wales, staying in a tiny caravan with them, all squashed like sardines in a tin, I am vulnerable to their whims. Our leader and his wife are in the caravan next door and generally keep watch over us, but they're not around for the little things, the petty things, the 'give me your sweets' things and 'last one in is a ninny!' jibe and the whispering and laughing behind my back.

Kathleen's not so bad, she's just a year older than me and her sister Mary and Paula her friend are fifteen years old, that makes them practically adults, or so they say! They said I look like I'm scrubbed clean everyday and I clean my teeth! What's so bad about that? I just shrugged it off when they made fun of me. I don't know what I'm supposed to do to please them. Well I know one thing- they love my stories. Every night before we go to sleep they ask me to tell them a ghost story. I like them liking my stories but what they don't know is that they are real; I mean from my own experience. I don't think they would like it if they knew the truth. They would treat me like some kind of weirdo, well more than they do now.

At school on my first day, I made the mistake of sitting at their dinner table and they tried to get rid of me, but the teacher on duty made me sit down in Mary's place and told them off for making a noise. They didn't like me intruding in their secret gang and every day that first week I had to sit in Mary's place and they hated it! Girls can be so cruel!

I am relieved that not all of them travel on the same school bus as me. Mary and Kathleen live in a village further out of town but Paula lives in a village near mine and often sits alone on the bus learning Spanish verbs. She is very intelligent and good at Spanish. I have a close friend who is a fellow rebel and we devised a method of secretly passing our school bus passes to each other if one of us forgot it. Leigh would sit in the seat in front of me and as there was a gap at the back of the seat, it was easy to pass the wallet through the hole. When the conductor came she would fumble in her satchel searching for it and then I would pass mine through to her- it worked every time! Sometimes we would make fun of Paula behind her back, I suppose it was my way of getting revenge for her nastiness towards me.

Things changed a little bit by bit. I come from a sporty, musical family. I don't really like sport but I am a fast sprinter developed by racing through a crowded town each morning to avoid being humiliated and caned by the head junior school teacher. Back then I won all my races and broke school records. The gang likes this and I can even say that on sporting occasions they are pleased to be associated with me. They came to accept me because of my running ability and also because I play the piano and play the hymns in morning assembly and have special permission to practice during break times, so I don't have to go out in the cold. They come into the music room when it suits them, saying that they have permission to practice singing with me. It's not true, but I don't mind really, except when they get bored and start poking around in the percussion cupboard and messing with the instruments and making a mess of the hymn sheets.

We all joined the Drama Club and became heavily involved in the school production of 'Toad of Toad Hall'- in fact Kathleen played little Mole, Paula was Ratty and Mary was the Washerwoman, while I was Chief Weasel. Then we all joined the Mountaineering Club. It's just the four of us on this Welsh trip and although they accept me as a menial member of the gang, being the youngest, I am still a target for their fun. That is of course until I have something unique to offer-my bed time ghost stories. Three nights in a row I have entertained them with a strange tale and being safely tucked into our sleeping bags, it is easy to take them on a scary journey and easy for me to enter into the scene, as I am just recalling what has actually happened to me.

It is the fourth day and we are climbing a very steep, high mountain. The freezing wind is thrashing and beating into our faces. My anorak is an old army cast-off and doesn't offer much shelter or warmth. I also suffer from asthma and stabbing pains are growing in my chest as I fight my way up the incline. I battle inwardly, not allowing my inner struggle to show. Somehow I tap into an inner energy, a strength from within which propels me forwards and up the extreme mountain slope. I take my mind off the pain by thinking about what story I am going to tell the gang tonight and strangely something comes into my head just as I am steadying myself with both hands on the earthy ridge. From below the ground a metal, magnetic force rattles my hands and I envisage an ugly, elf-like creature, buried below, struggling to get free.

Momentarily I stand steadying myself as the others pass by and I wonder if I am hallucinating. I get the impression of a grotesque little man squirming and squealing like a piglet under the ground. I focus my attention and send my energy like an x-ray force through the earth. He stops squirming and is thrilled to make contact with me. He pitifully explains that he has been buried for hundreds of years by a sorcerer and that if I let him out he will be of use to me. I don't know how to free him, but he assures me that all I have to do is use my inner strength and say the words with feeling, 'let Rimple free'. I don't know why I feel sorry for him or why I even agree to let him out-but I do! I say the words with feeling and sure enough a dark energy springs from below the damp earth. "Now you have your story for tonight! " He affirms gruffly," and leave the rest to me!"

I catch up with the others who are resting by a collection of rocks other climbers have built into a little tower and they're eating their sandwiches with red, frozen hands. I can't believe what has just happened- it was almost like Aladdin freeing the Genii from an old lamp, except that I wasn't granted three wishes, although he did say he would be useful to me, but I ponder how? His liberation is a secret between him and me and affords me new-found confidence. The pain in my chest has faded and I feel much better. Even if the encounter was a daydream or a figment of my imagination, the idea of it gives me strength and somehow I have an advantage over the others. For the first time I am in control and not fearful of their teasing or taunting. For the first time I have the upper hand.

The descent isn't as difficult as the ascent and we soon make good timing back for our last night in the caravan. We are all going to eat together for our last supper and our leader's wife is cooking bangers and mash. There is ginger sponge pudding in two large cans which are to be cooked on our little gas cooker. We sit outside around a crackling bonfire and watch tiny sparks shoot off into the dark night. The gang are happy and I am relieved to have survived the ordeal of the trip and in fact I am happy in the moment, feeling a sense of community and friendship, especially as the leader plays his guitar and we all join in melancholy folk songs. Just as we are hammering out the 'If I had a hammer song ', there is an almighty explosion from our caravan and the leader runs inside. "Ok, who was in charge of the pudding?" he inquires angrily. Mary and Paula sheepishly put their hands up. "Looks like you didn't put enough water in the saucepan girls and the tins have exploded all over the place. Get it cleaned up!"

And that is the end of our lovely evening. Kathleen and I help the two older girls to wash down all the surfaces. The treacly sponge has blasted everywhere. We find large pieces encrusted on the roof and thousands of tiny balls of sponge stuck in the smallest cracks and crannies, there are even bits in our sleeping bags. It takes ages to clean.

Eventually, tired and exhausted we flop into our sleeping bags. My heart is fluttering as I want them to ask for a story and it seems they might be too tired, but Kathleen, who is the kindest, asks for the last story of the trip and I am only too happy to oblige. The story goes like this:

'Once upon a time, a very long time ago in the land of Green Ginger lived a tyrant, a terrible ruler who was really a sorcerer. His people were terrified of him and lived in fear of being turned to stone or buried alive. His Kingdom was not an ordinary Empire because it dwelt in the Fairy Realm where it was hidden from human prying eyes. Elves, Pixies, Kelpies and tiny woodland folk abided in the forest and kept secret hideouts to escape from the Sorcerer who had strange, ugly deformed helpers to wait on him and do his dirty work. One such helper was a hideous, ogre-type creature called Rimple whose job was to keep account of the Sorcerer's gold.

One day when Rimple was counting the Sorcerer's golden coins, one rolled away off the table and tumbled out of the palace, along the footpath into a rabbit's warren. Rimple tried to climb inside the burrow but he kept slipping and sliding backwards. He was making such a noise that he alerted the Sorcerer who went to investigate the disturbance. Rimple tried to explain what had happened but the Sorcerer having no patience with incompetent idiots, threw him into the rabbit warren and sealed up the entrance saying 'there you will remain until an earthly child releases you!" The sorcerer was certain that no earthly child would ever free him. But one day when a group of girls were climbing in the very spot where Rimple had been buried and the youngest, who was following behind the others, planted both hands on the ground to steady herself, she suddenly felt movement below the earth and heard someone shouting and screaming for help like a suckling piglet. The girl felt sorry for the creature and listened to Rimple's story. She wanted to set him free so she repeated the words' let Rimple free' and he was liberated. In return he promised to help the girl.

He followed the gang all the way back to their caravan and watched them having fun around their camp fire. He watched and waited. Then he began his magical tricks by exploding tins of treacle sponge all over their tiny caravan...'

I finish the story abruptly as an almighty crash shakes the little caravan like a terrifying earthquake. The caravan door flings open and thrashes against the metal side banging and clanging and everyone shrieks and screams and hides inside their sleeping bags. Everyone except me as I watch in awe at the unfolding horror. Bashing and crashing resound from the roof as though someone with iron boots is jumping up and down attempting to get in. Lightning flashes across the windows and lights up the inside of the caravan. The girls are terrified and continue screeching. Mary calls for help and for someone to close the door. They are all petrified except me. I am enjoying the crying and squealing. A whirlwind rushes around the tiny cabin shaking everything in its wake and the girls howl uncontrollably. I get up to close the door. I am not afraid. The door is difficult to close and the lightning flashes across my face but I stand firm and close the door. Then the onslaught stops. All is quiet. No one says a word. They peer out from under their hiding holes staring at me in horror and wonder. They think I am brave to be the only one to get up and close the door and scared of me because in my story the monster in the mountain comes down to terrorize the girls and it came true!

Little did they know that Rimple had kept his promise and disappeared?

After this incident in the caravan, the girls never make fun of me again, or tease or taunt me, in fact, in their eyes- I am superwoman!

⸻⬦⬥⬦⸻

EBONY ELEPHANT

"Come in! Come in my dear!" enthuses Mrs. Dalwimple. "Your teacher said you would come and collect these things for your jumble sale."

I step inside her prestigious apartment full of amazing memorabilia. Her husband was a Colonel in the British Army serving in India and her walls are lined with Indian mementos from that era.

"Would you like a cup of tea, or juice?" she enquires graciously, "or whatever you young teenage girls drink nowadays; is it coffee?"

"Er, no thank you, I have to get back as the school bus is waiting to take the collection." I answer politely lifting the box full of nick-knacks from a delicate, ornate table. On top of the bric-a-brac is a small, black elephant. "Ah he is so sweet!"

"Indeed!" Adds Mrs. Dalwimple as she picks up the ebony elephant and places it in my coat pocket. "There, he is yours now. Take care of him; he is very special."

I nod thanking her and hurry back to the school bus to join the others who have been in the area collecting boxes of cast-offs for our jumble sale in aid of Live Aid.

After school on my way home, I feel something in my coat pocket, forgetting that the elephant was planted there and am surprised to see his little smiling face gazing up at me. I love elephants and he is so cute. I hold him in the palm of my hand and a warmth glides up my arm. I am happy with my gift and decide to put him on my bedside table.

Later that evening, before I go to sleep, I gaze at the endearing little ebony elephant standing under my bedside lamp and I notice for the first time, he has little ivory tusks and as I pick him up to inspect him, an electric vibration spreads up my arm, radiating heat into my chest, almost like hugging a hot water bottle. I lie down and hold him close to my heart and close my eyes. Immediately a scene unfolds, like watching a movie and a young female voice speaks:-

"It is dark and I am alone in a strange place. I am sad because everything around me is unfamiliar and different and not what I expected. I am engaged to an eccentric young man whose English Aristocratic family live in India and are close friends with the Viceroy. I understand I have been invited to visit them by way of being vetted to see if I am worthy to marry their son. My family are working class and I have lived in a small farming village with no knowledge or experience of high society etiquette, in fact I am the first person in my village to go to University in London, which is where I met my fiancé and how I came to be here, alone in a foreign country where everything is totally alien. I had expected support from Unwin, my fiancé, but in his family's home he has become distant, unloving, cold and indifferent. I think his family don't approve of our intended marriage. They don't like my modern clothes and my jeans. They don't approve of my free flowing long hair, trailing over my shoulders, hippy style, which they think is unkempt and undignified. They want me to dress like Princess Anne and in fact they wanted Unwin to marry Princess Anne!

I didn't expect to be billeted away from the house, tucked out of sight from the rest of the family in an annex. It is my first night in India and I am used to being with Unwin but now I am alone and afraid, scared of the unknown night sounds, and uncomfortable in the intense heat. The mosquito net surrounding my bed is strange, but I have been warned about treacherous mosquito bites and their dire consequences. I sit up listening to the sound of maracas played distinctly through my open window, shaking a unique Latin rhythm, inciting me to tap my feet to the syncopated beat, which momentarily alleviates my anxiety; but then I remember Unwin explaining about the grasshoppers rubbing their legs together at night making the sound of percussive maracas and I shiver at the thought, as I hate insects. I want to laugh at my stupidity, but hot tears roll down my cheeks. I don't want to cry. I don't want to feel sorry for myself, but I am isolated and so lonely. I look up and there is the most magical, most enchanting vision I have ever seen. Is it a beautiful fairy, red, golden and buzzing electric-yellow? I watch mesmerized by its captivating gentle dance in the blackness haloed by its brilliant light and then I also remember that Unwin had spoken about 'fireflies'. I lie down and fight my fears until sleep engulfs me."

The vision ends and I place the elephant back on my bedside table and turn off the light. It was so real and the sadness and fear of the woman was intense. Eventually, I fall asleep and the world takes care of itself in my normal routine existence.

A few weeks go by and I am busy revising for exams and going to dance classes and piano lessons and I forget about the ebony elephant. I receive a message from my teacher asking me to visit Mrs. Dalwimple as she specifically asked for me to collect more jumble, so here I am ringing her bell. She opens the door enthusiastically and asks me to enter. As I follow her through the hallway I note that some of her paintings are missing and she doesn't seem to have as many valuable antiques on display. She notices me observing the gaps on the wall and nonchalantly states; "time my dear to get rid of the past. There's too much clutter around. Time to sort things out!"

She leads me into her sitting room where she has arranged two plates and a lovely iced cake and so I can't refuse her hospitality and sit down with her to eat a slice. She asks about the ebony elephant and I tell her he is quite happy on my bedside table. We talk a little about the weather and then unexpectedly she folds into a story..."It is dark and I am alone in a strange place..."

She speaks the exact same words which echoed in my head the night when I held the elephant and the exact same scene unfolds almost as if I am there again.

When she finishes she smiles as though nothing happened and I can't finish my cake because I am too shocked and make an excuse to take the bag of jumble and exit quickly. As I leave she shouts, "Be sure to come back my dear!"

That evening I ponder the incident at Mrs. Dalwimple's and wonder if another vision might transpire if I hold the elephant next to my chest. As I pick him up I notice more detail etched on his back which I hadn't seen previously and his smile isn't so wide as before, but maybe I am wrong? I dare myself to close my eyes to see if another scene unfolds and sure enough I am there, back in India and the female voice speaks;

"I have a small primitive bathroom next to my bedroom. It looks like a cowshed from back home and has a cold tap perched on top of a lead pipe. The water runs into a basin and when unplugged, it runs into a metal gulley and trickles all the way around the room into a drain, similar to the watershed where the calves are housed on the farm. The family have made it clear that my short skirts and flimsy dresses are not appropriate to wear in the conservative English community in the Nilgiris Hills in South India. They have employed their tailor to make me some suitable clothes as they wish me to appear and behave like Princess Anne. The bathroom is adequate with a large window looking out to massive Eucalyptus trees where myriads of monkeys scatter and chatter, fighting, playing and throwing garbage into the garden. They are not cute or adorable but aggressive and a nuisance. I enter the bathroom and almost have a heart attack. There is a gross, huge monkey sitting in my window, sucking my toothpaste out of the tube. I scream and run out and one of the servants comes to my aid and shoos away the monkey explaining that-"Missy Sahib, it is happening all the times. Do not be worrying!" The vision fades and I am left shaking from the experience. Sleep is difficult but I place the elephant back in its position and quiet descends.

The next morning I am curious about the incident and decide to call on Mrs. Dalwimple. She opens the door and looks a little frail but is pleased to see me. Again I note that more paintings from the hallway have disappeared and she has even less antiques on display. I follow her into the sitting room which is a little cold and she offers to put on the heating but I assure her I am fine. She says she has nothing to offer me but asks about the elephant and without warning she begins to relate the second story about the monkey in the bathroom. Just as she easily slipped into the scene she slips out of it again without showing any signs of having done so. Somehow the time just doesn't seem right to ask her about the elephant's magical properties and I don't stay long, but promise to visit again soon.

That evening I can't wait to try out the elephant again to see what unfolds next and make an excuse to go to bed early. As I pick up the elephant I notice more detail on the little fella. His tail is longer with a bushy tassel engraved on the end. I quickly enter the trance and find myself at dinner with Unwin's family and the voice explains;-

"Their British 'stiff upper lip' attitude is apparent at all times. In their Aristocratic evening wear they sit at the large dining table engaged in polite conversation. I am wearing my long hair tied up in a bun on the top of my head, but this apparently is offensive to the family as the Sikh male community wear their hair in the same fashion. My long nylon dress, which is actually a nightdress, is not suitable in the heat and is sticking to my body. As usual I am uncomfortable enduring the family's gaze and scrutiny. I have become accustomed to their ways and try to please wherever possible, but I am struggling to be accepted. It seems that the more I try to be one of them, the more things go wrong. I am still fearful of all the strange insects, animals and creatures which patrol the Indian night and earlier when a mongoose ran under the sofa I was terrified and made a spectacle of myself by screaming and jumping up on a chair, whilst the family continued nonplussed, drinking their cocktails.

I hate the geckoes who hide behind pictures on the wall and one in particular who lives behind a painting over my bed. I loathe the way they zip out their long red tongues to catch flies and insects. They run all over the ceiling and in fact there are a few roaming around this evening, darting in and out of the light fittings. Sathu, the kitchen servant brings in a huge silver tureen of soup and places it in the middle of the table. Just as he is about to position the ladle in the soup, something lands with a great crash in the middle of the hot, steaming liquid, splashing soup all over the clean table cloth. A lizard has just shed its tail into the soup and no one is perturbed. No one even flinches. Unwin's mother orders another tureen of soup explaining; "it's only a lizard tail my dear! It happens all the time; one gets used to it!"

I don't think I'll ever get used to it or the night terrors where two species of ants cover my white marble bedroom floor at night to fight for territory. It's a nightmare as the whole area becomes one undulating mass of black insect battleground. The heat is unbearable and so I sleep naked and the other night I was in bed trying to sleep but overcome with a horrid itching sensation all over my body and when I fought through my mosquito net to turn on the side lamp, I discovered to my horror that I was being eaten alive by tiny red ants which had nested in my bed! I shrieked and screamed and was rescued by a female servant who took me to another room. I will never get over the shock of the infestation and the ants all over my body. The servant hosed me down with cold water and took care of me. I want to go home!"

The scene evaporates and I am back in the moment in my bedroom shaking with horror at the vision of being eaten alive by tiny red ants. It makes me feel itchy and paranoid about insects. Poor Mrs. Dalwimple – she must have felt so isolated. Eventually I fall asleep dreaming of geckoes and invasive ants!

Exams and more exams take up my time revising and preparing for them and I don't have time to venture into the elephant visions, until one afternoon, tired after an early morning exam, I flop down on my bed and happen to see the little ebony elephant with a carved teardrop in one eye. I pick him up and examine his face. I know for definite this new feature was not there before. I stroke his tear and almost immediately fall into a vision and the female voice narrates.

"I am attending a prestigious Indian wedding. The Maharaja of Porbunda's daughter is getting married and as Unwin's family are close friends, we are invited to the three day event. Unwin and I, as newly- weds, have to appear particularly finely attired and Unwin's Mother has arranged her famous dress designer to make me three amazing outfits to wear each day. I have to say I love them and no money has been spared in the making of the designer clothes.

For the first day I am wearing a mogul style outfit in burnt orange with gold thread. The pantaloons fit beautifully and the overcoat is enchanting and although Unwin's parents at first didn't approve, they have come to accept me. I have learnt to be more refined and have settled into the aristocratic high society mode of life. I didn't know what to expect of marriage and I am not unhappy, but there is something missing. We have fallen into a routine way of living, but I had hoped to feel more alive.

At the first evening's bonfire, I stand alone watching the flames rise high into the black night. Everyone has feasted and for the first time I have eaten real gold. Beaten flakes of real gold adorned little celebratory cakes and it was an amazing experience. Beside me in the crowd, I feel a presence. A strong masculine charisma stands beside me. I look into his eyes and he mine. For a few moments everything vanishes and only he and I exist. He smiles and I smile back, not able to resist his charm. He asks if I want a drink and leads me into the bar, suggesting that my husband is not taking good care of me and that if he was in such a position, he would not leave me unattended. I am embarrassed and touched by his concern for me, realising that Unwin is lacking in his general care of me. Somehow we talk all night, lost in each other's ways and I drink three gin and tonics, which according to Unwin's family is a crime and most unacceptable in polite society to drink in the company of a stranger- not even an English stranger! When Unwin eventually collects me I am flushed and very happy, looking forward to seeing my new-found friend the next day at the second round of wedding rituals.

For the second day my outfit is as stunning as the first. A white Swiss silk blouse with beautiful long sleeves is the base underneath a chique bolero in green and real gold thread with a matching layered skirt. It is almost a Spanish gypsy outfit and I imagine myself playing a role in Bizet's Carmen. The second day of the wedding is more ritually symbolic with all kinds of ancient ceremonies performed by the immediate families. As I stand watching a scarf tied around the happy couple, I feel someone close by who makes my heart flutter and the palms of my hand sweat in anticipation of our meeting. He stands by my side and we talk and laugh. I tell him the family was not pleased I had drunk three gin and tonics and he scoffs at their petty attitude and insists we imbibe some more. Feeling guilty, I agree. At the bar we meet some other Indian officers from the army and one asks to speak with my friend in private and he orders another soldier to take care of me in his absence.

"I see you are acquainted with the Prince?" he queries. I am dumbfounded as I had no idea of his royal blood, but I don't reveal my true feelings and continue a conversation about the wedding. When the Prince returns I am a little cautious and he senses my reticence to further our conversation. I explain I didn't realise he was an Indian Prince and he laughs. He warns me that we are being closely watched and that our behaviour is unacceptable in both his society and mine. A marriage has been arranged for him and will take place in a few months and it is thought unseemly for him to be openly flirting with me and I, as an English married lady, drinking with him am committing a serious social, insensitive offence. I apologise for my ignorance but he takes my arm and asks, "Do you believe in destiny?" I nod and he continues, "My marriage is arranged and it's something I have to do, rather than want to do. Do you understand?" I nod again. "I am sorry I have been called away. Tomorrow we will meet at the ball and with your permission we will dance!" He kisses my hand and our eyes meet in secret longing.

For the ball, my dress is beautiful and very daring. Simonis the famous dress designer, has created a beautiful long flowing ball gown in silk. It is the colour of a calm sea with delicate swirls of springtime green. I am a little shy displaying the low cut décolletage of my ball gown but Simonis says-"If you have it flaunt it!" I cover my shoulders with a lovely shawl and enter the ballroom, hoping to see the Prince. Everyone is there but I can't see him. Unwin leads me over to a small group of prestigious high society Indian folk, one of whom, Rani, is a famous dancer and she is jealous of me. She instinctively senses my shyness about my low-cut gown and rips away my shawl in a brazen sweep. I feel naked and exposed in front of everyone, but I do not show any sign of embarrassment and smile as I walk away proudly to the balcony. I know I have committed a social indelicate crime by meeting with the Prince and Rani wished to publicly shame me, but she did not succeed! While Unwin joins his friends, I wait anxiously for the Prince to appear but his close friend surreptitiously warns me that the Prince has been ordered to be on duty and he is sorry he can't meet. The friend whispers-"You see they are watching, they must intervene" and with that he bows and disappears.

The scene fades and I am left with a deep sense of loss. I am only a young school girl without experience of such intense, passionate feelings but I understand her disappointment. I decide to take a walk to Mrs. Dalwimple's to find out what happened to the Prince, for I am now profoundly involved in the story and need to know more.

Mrs. Dalwimple, as always is pleased to see me, but is more frail than usual and her hallway is now almost deplete of all fine paintings and artefacts. It is quite chilly in her apartment and she is wrapped in a blanket. We sit down in her sitting room which is also becoming quite sparsely furnished and I ask her about the Prince.

She pauses momentarily, then smiles realizing that the elephant has told me all saying, "He was the one true love of my life. Our passion for each other was so intense like the meeting of soul-spirits, but we never saw each other again. When Unwin and I returned to London he spent most of his time away at University in Yorkshire and I stayed with his aunt in London. The Prince with his newly wed wife came to London looking for me and even visited aunt's flat and had tea, but unfortunately I was teaching and never got to see them. The rest of my life I yearned to see him. Such is fate my dear!"

I was sad when I returned home after learning about Mrs. Dalwimple's unrequited love and resolved to keep visiting her to keep her company.

Today is Tuesday and we have finished all our exams and this afternoon I will visit Mrs. Dalwimple. When the door opens a younger woman answers and I explain I have visited previously to collect jumble sale bric-a-brac. "Ah that must have been Mrs. Slater, the housekeeper you met, who stayed here for a while after my Mother died. She took care of selling things and gradually emptied the flat ready to be sold."

I am totally shocked and am lost for words. "But I spoke to Mrs. Dalwimple just the other day?" I question.

"I'm sorry my dear, you must be mistaken, as I explained she died a while back!"

As I turn around to leave I spy an old photograph lying at the foot of the stairs- "Ah yes, that's my mother!" says the woman as she picks up the photograph to show me. The photo is Mrs. Dalwimple. I would recognise her anywhere and in her hands she is holding a little ebony elephant.

UNCONDITIONAL LOVE

The most wonderful thing in life is 'to love and be loved' -our teacher reads to the class and we all agree it's a pretty nice thing to say, but at the age of twelve, well nearly thirteen, I mean, it's words, just words really! I look around the class and I don't think there's anyone who has ever been 'in love' well Tilly says she's in love with Gareth, but then she changes her mind because Gareth loves football more than her and Jeremy says he's in love with Lady Ga Ga-well honestly it will be Taylor Swift next month. I suppose we all love our parents and they love us back, but does that count?

Our teacher talks about 'love' because we are supposed to be doing Romeo and Juliette and he has chosen Betty Broadmore to play the lead part, only because she has flowing long, blonde hair and big baby blue eyes and wears loads of make –up and all she has to do is flash her eyelashes at Mr. Broadmore and she gets away with murder! She can't act- well I don't think she can!

"Romeo, Romeo, wherefore art thou Romeo?" She says those lines without any feeling and with a load of bubble gum stuck in her pouty mouth. I can play Juliette much better than her and when I practice at home in front of my mirror, I can almost feel the audience swoon at my performance.

Mr Broadmore has chosen Johnny Blake to play Romeo, only because he's the tallest in the class and the costume fits him better than anyone else. Personally I think he's gay and isn't in the least interested in Betty. He likes Jasper, the football captain, so the chemistry between Romeo and Juliette isn't there; but old Broady can't see it!

On and on old Broady sings snippets from old songs, 'love lifts us up where we belong...', 'love, love me do...' and 'love is a many splendid thing...' I don't think many of us are listening. Jack is playing a game on his phone under the desk, Martha is drawing dinosaurs in her diary and Josh is texting his girlfriend on his phone which is hidden behind his large pencil case. Me? Well I'm just day dreaming because tonight when I go home Dad is bringing our new puppy and I can't wait to see her. She is a pure pedigree Blue Rhone Cocker Spaniel.

Dinky, Dinky she is so beautiful and cute. I love her. I think she loves me too. She is the sweetest puppy you have ever seen. Her paws are too big for her little body and she pads up and down the sitting-room carpet so pleased with herself. I think she is happy to be in a loving home and she likes her new basket loaded with lots of toys. I think her favourite is the squeaky turtle. I want her to sleep on my bed but Dad says she has to stay downstairs, but I secretly think he likes having her to himself!

We all love Dinky so much and I can't imagine a time without her. She is growing daily and has become not just a pet, but a little character in her own right. She loves it when I come home from school and take her for a walk and play with her favourite ball in the park. Mr Broadmore has given the part of the Nurse to me. He says it's a very important role and as I'm so bossy I will do it well! I would sooner be Juliette but I suppose I can make the part interesting. Perhaps give her an Italian accent-I'm good at accents!

It's our performance next week and everyone is nervous. Betty still hasn't learnt all her lines and Johnny doesn't want to kiss her! Old Broady won't let me do an Italian accent for the Nurse because he says the others aren't doing accents so it won't fit. So I suggest maybe a soft Scottish accent but he said, 'definitely not!' Anyway we're going on holiday after the show and that will be nice except that Dad has arranged for Dinky to be put in kennels for a week and I don't think she will like it, in fact I know she will hate it!

The show is going great and it suddenly came to me whilst standing idly on stage as Miss Juliette spouts her speech, I might do a little dusting around her and tidying up, as her Nurse would do. I could see some members in the audience appreciated what I was trying to do as they were smiling, but old Broady in the interval tells me I am not to pull focus and bring attention to myself. So in the second Act I decide to react to Juliette a little more, by flailing my arms around and making faces, but Broady didn't like that either. Now we are getting lots of applause so I think it all went well!

Holidays are fine, but I'm missing Dinky- my heart hurts. I love her so much! I miss cuddling into her soft fur which smells of puppyness. I love and miss our playtime together. She is always happy and she makes me happy too.

Dad picks up Dinky from the kennels on our way home and although she is pleased to see us, something is wrong. Something is different. Dad and I have a special relationship with her and I know he notices too. As she snuggles into my chest I feel her nose is a little warm and her smell has changed. At home she is not hungry. She flops into her basket and doesn't want to play. My heart is heavy and I am not hungry either. I sit by her basket stroking her head and Dad is upset. By ten o'clock, I should have gone to bed, but she is really poorly and Dad calls the vet. On the phone I hear Dad pleading with him to come; he even agrees to pay extra charges for the night visit.

She has caught Distemper from the kennels and the vet has given her lots of medicine. Dad walks the vet back to his car and stays outside for a while. His head is down and he looks upset. When he comes in he says she will get better and that he will stay by her side to give her the medicine throughout the night. I don't want to leave her but I am made to go to bed.

In the morning she seems a little better and I feel ok to go to school, although it is very difficult to concentrate on love poems when is she is so ill. Mr.

Broadmore has a new favourite and asks Shona Newton to read the juicy bits in the poems, as I think Betty's Juliette was not that impressive and if truth be known old Broady was disappointed at her performance. I could have told him so!

I open the door at home and there is silence. There is no pitter-patter of furry pads on the tiled floor and no tail wagging. Dinky is lying in her basket and her breathing is heavy and irregular. Dad has not left her side all day and has not gone to work. He hugs me and says she may not pull through. "No, no, no! You can't let her die, you can't!" I cry. I hold her close and my tears fall on her face and she tries to lick them off her nose. I love her so much and she loves me!

Dad does not leave her side and stays with her all night again. In the morning her basket has gone and so has Dad. My heart is broken and I won't go to school. My world is shattered and I can't imagine life without Dinky. I am bereft without her. Nothing will ever be the same.

Everyone says life goes on and we have to live life to the full, but my life is half empty without Dinky. Dad is quiet and doesn't say much. Mum says we can have another dog but neither of us want that. The days are passing and I have her photograph by my bedside. I remember her every night. At school we now have to write an essay on 'Love' and our feelings about it and I am going to write about Dinky because I loved her and she loved me.

Dad is different this morning. He is smiling and calls me out into the garden to tell me something which he doesn't want Mum to hear. His eyes are glistening and his voice is shaky as he says:

"Last night your Mum and I had an argument, so I went downstairs to sleep on the sofa. I fell asleep and was woken by a sloppy, wet tongue licking my face!"

My heart is pounding. I can hardly wait for him to finish what he is saying.

"I opened my eyes and Dinky was staring at me. She was licking my face and hands to thank me for taking care of her. She showed me she is still around! My love she is still around!"

My Dad is a no-nonsense Army man and does not deal in fantasy and I know he is telling the truth. I know she is still around and he and I feel her. She will not leave us.

I am doing some research for my essay on pet dogs and I found a scientific fact:-

"there is scientific evidence that when we look into our dog's eyes, oxytocin (love hormone) is released and when they gaze back, it's released in their eyes too." Isn't that wonderful?

I begin my essay-'there is love and there is love and there is nothing like the unconditional love of a pet for its owner and owner for their pet. A dog in particular asks for nothing in return except to 'love and be loved'...

IT REALLY DID HAPPEN!

The desks are set out in the hall and I note there are extra clocks to remind us when the exam starts and finishes. 'Written English Exam' is marked on the white board in large black letters-as if we need reminding? We take our places and prepare our pens like swords ready for a dual…'remember the pen is mightier than the sword' our English teacher claims and I want to laugh, as the moment is so serious and Mr. Saunders is marching up and down twitching his nose like an Easter bunny on parade!

"And begin…" Mr. Saunders declares dramatically staring at his stop-watch and we're off with a fluttering of paper, shuffling of feet and nervous coughing from the front row. I am eager to find out the title of the essay as Miss Braithwaite said there are over half marks for this assignment and I like writing stories. She said not to be afraid of going over the top with our imagination and making the action vivid with colourful imagery.

I scroll through the first part of the paper, which isn't too difficult, and race to the second page to find the title of the essay written in big bold letters-'IT REALLY DID HAPPEN!' The title is right up my street, as I have a wealth of experiences to choose from which most people would find hard to believe. I just have to find the right way to write about the subject. For a few moments I wonder which story to tell and pause to look at the clock. I have plenty of time left to describe a happening which no one is going to believe, in fact I have trouble believing it myself, yet I know it really happened...

It was on the eve of my eighth birthday and I was excited because I was hoping to receive the book I most wanted in all the world-Alice in Wonderland. I loved fairy stories and fantasy tales and in my home there were no books to read, only newspapers and Dad used most of those to light the fire. I had been given a few story books for Christmas and birthdays but I had been told that on my eighth birthday I would be too old to read fairy stories and that I had to be grown up and not waste my time idly reading nonsense. I wanted to be eight years old but I was upset to think that I had to stop reading fairy stories. Suddenly outside my bedroom door, on the landing, I heard the most beautiful music. It was a haunting melody played on a flute. I closed my eyes and saw a beautiful winged fairy sitting on the bannister with her legs crossed playing a little wooden recorder. I was lost in her enchanting tune and heard the words-"You are never too old to believe in magic!"

The music gradually faded and her words remained in my head-"You are never too old to believe in magic." I knew this in my heart and resolved that even if they took away my story books I would find a way of secretly reading all the fairy stories in the world. Night closed in and I fell asleep with the haunting, beautiful melody of the fairy flute playing in my mind.

'Now here is the peculiar happening. I woke very early in the morning on my eighth birthday and lay awake hoping I was going to get the book 'Alice in Wonderland' from my parents, when I heard an odd sound. In my mind's eye I could see skipping up the stairs in a very jolly manner a mop and a brush dancing up the stairs side by side. The mop looked like our ordinary mop but it had stick-like arms and little stick legs. The mop head tassels sprang up and down as it pranced up the stairs. It had a very feminine appearance and the brush, a masculine aura with its brown strong bristles standing on end like an American crew cut. He also had stick-like arms and legs. They bounced up to my room and came in through the door without opening it. I sat up in bed staring at them, horrified. Then they suddenly leapt on my bed, laughing and giggling like mischievous school children saying- "you'll never be too old for magic and fun!" and they took my arms, one in each of their stick-like appendages and flew me around the room. High on the ceiling and round and round they flung me. I was distressed and felt sick and begged them to stop, which they did after a while and they couldn't understand why I didn't like it, but it was horrible and shocking. I mean a brush and a mop had come to life and I wasn't sure whether they were good or bad beings. I didn't want any more of their tricks and they were most disappointed that I didn't enjoy their treat. I was not dreaming and the experience was all too real. They seemed hurt that I wasn't in the mood for fun and games with a mop and a brush, so they left me alone in the room pondering what had happened. I felt sick from the dizziness as flying around the room made me nauseous. Then I heard my Father get up and go downstairs. He was always up early and made breakfast. My legs were wobbly as I walked into the kitchen and to my horror the mop and brush were there by the door. They were never left in the kitchen but had a place in the outhouse. I looked terrified at them and was afraid to sit down, but my Father made me sit at the table to eat and there by my plate was a present. It was a book- 'Alice in Wonderland' and I was overjoyed to receive it. I looked up towards the mop and brush and they seemed to smile and almost do a little jig!"

I know my story is too fantastical to believe, but honestly it really did happen, I'm not kidding!'

Mr. Saunders states officiously, "Pens down!" and with a great ricochet clatter of pens on desks we all breathe again. As I hand in my paper I hope Miss Braithwaite will like my story but I doubt whether she will understand that it really happened. At lunch time I meet up with my friends who think the English exam wasn't too bad, but most had difficulty making up stories for the essay.

"Well, I made up a story about a pet dragon who liked eating tomatoes!" states Jack, eating a tomato from his lunch box.

"That's lame!" asserts Vicky carefully spreading a sachet of mayonnaise on her lettuce. "Mine was about a dinosaur and a space ship- what about you?" She questions, pointing a wooden fork in my direction.

"Me? Well er.. I wrote about a mop and brush!" I utter, taking a sip of sparkling water from the bottle and everyone laughs, thinking I'm joking but when they realise I'm being utterly honest they become silent and I wonder why they find it so strange to accept that a mop and brush can be the subject of a good story.

In class Miss Braithwaite discusses the exam and goes over the first section of answers and I am relieved that my score was good and she promises to have the essays marked by next week and then holds an open forum for us to ask any questions about our essays and Jake asks," What do you think about Aliens miss, I mean do you really think they exist?"

"Research is the answer Jake, research. There are reliable sources who state categorically that Aliens do exist and that they are here amongst us, in fact the American Government has been officially tasked to reveal evidence locked in vaults for many years, as proof of American co-operation with different species of Alien."

"Ooh Miss, do you think Derek is an Alien? He looks like one!" adds Carl who pulls a silly face and the class laugh at his antics.

"Now don't let's be silly or unkind Carl, we're talking quite seriously about the topic Jake introduced and unless you have anything interesting or factual about the subject, I suggest you keep quiet?"

Miriam shyly puts up her hand and the class turn to look at her as she hardly ever speaks and Miss Braithwaite encourages her to talk- "Well Miss, I was reading the other day..."

"Oooh!" Interrupts a few silly boys.

"Continue Miriam and those boys making the silly noise are now on detention. I know who they are and they can see me after class!" Asserts Miss Braithwaite giving the boys one of her looks.

"Well Miss I read that some humans belong to different species of Alien who come from other planets and the people who are here on earth don't always know that they belong to an Alien family far away and that sometimes the Alien family come in disguise or take on different forms of life in order to communicate with their Alien family member."

"No way?" Exclaims Tony, "You mean like your cat could be your Alien Dad?"

Everyone laughs, except me and Miss Braithwaite and she urges Miriam to continue.

"Miss, I read that Aliens can take on almost any form they wish, it doesn't have to be a living creature; it can even be an inanimate object!"

The class discuss silly ideas about objects turning into Aliens and Vicky pipes up asking, "What about a mop and brush Miss, can they be Aliens?"

I turn away and look out of the window. I don't want to talk about my experience and be ridiculed by the whole class and I am glad when the bell goes to release us all into the noisy corridor.

A week later our exam sheets are handed back and I am relieved to know I did well but Miss Braithwaite asks me to see her at the end of the class and I am worried. I can't concentrate on the lesson as my mind keeps attacking me with all sorts of problems which Miss Braithwaite might want to discuss and I am nervous about my essay and what she really thinks.

I am relieved when everyone disappears at the end of the lesson and Miss Braithwaite asks me to take a seat at her desk. She says in a sweet tone, "Don't worry, you haven't done anything wrong, in fact I want to congratulate you on top marks for your exam."

I sigh, thankful that all is well, but she looks seriously into my eyes and begins;" You mustn't feel upset, worried or alone. I loved your story and I believe you. I believe you because something similar happened to me when I was a child!"

Lesley Ann Eden

THINGS THAT GO CRASH IN THE NIGHT!

It's quite a common occurrence for people to hear strange noises in the dead of night or be woken by unfathomable thumps, knocks or even footsteps, but I bet not a lot of people have had their bed leg sawn in half by some invisible force whilst asleep? Well, I have! I keep the shattered piece of the bed leg to prove it. I even have photos. There is absolutely no reason how it happened or why- except that the next morning there was a massive outage across the whole world and everything came to a standstill, but apart from that there is no real connection or motive why I should have been chosen to experience such a traumatic attack.

All I know is that I was deeply asleep until my little dog Freddie, who sleeps on my bed, jumped off and then jumped back on again and the left side of my bed rose in the air! As I fully awoke I half sat up and felt the end of the bed rise by some invisible force. It was pitch –black so I couldn't see anything. It must have been around two 'clock in the early hours of a Friday morning when the end of the bed was lifted into the air. Freddie didn't bark or make a sound, which was most unusual. As the bed end elevated I was numb and devoid of all feeling. I wasn't shocked or surprised but then whoever or whatever was responsible for hoisting up the bed simply let it go and it crashed to the floor with a loud thud.

In the silent aftermath, I tried to understand what had happened, wondering how it could have occurred. My bed is a Louis 1Vth style bed which I have painted ornately to match the style of the period with gold scrolls and beautiful flowers carved into the wooden bedhead and it is a very strong sturdy bed. I treated myself to an expensive mattress the kind apparently astronauts use, with the same expensive pillows, so all in all there is nothing cheap or shoddy about my bed and there is no way that it could have elevated off the ground and smashed down by itself.

I wasn't afraid, just puzzled. There wasn't anything in the bedroom that was threatening me physically or menacing me in any way. In those strange moments of silent waiting nothing happened. The bed didn't seem unduly affected and I was able to lie down again, unharmed, but perplexed at the incident. At the time I didn't realize the extent of the damage and somehow managed to sleep until dawn when Freddie and I got up and it was then that I discovered the unbelievable damage. A quarter of the right leg had been severed in two and the stump was holding up that side of the bed. Somehow it didn't affect the overall balance. I closely examined the sawn-off piece and took photos of it. Nothing made any sense until I heard the news. There was an outage across the world. A cyber attack had knocked out communication across all countries and had affected everything including airports, banks, all industries and social media. Perhaps my whisperers were warning me that something massive was happening across the globe? But it still didn't explain why my bed had been targeted – was I being warned of something terrible about to happen? Was I sympathetic, empathetic, susceptible, vulnerable to magnetic energy pulsing through the atmosphere? I wondered why the world had to have a dark day and what was being hidden from everyone through the severed communication and questioned if it was a practice run for something more sinister?

I am afraid I have no answers and my bed remains the same. Perhaps I am content to leave it the way it was shattered, as a reminder that the world of the unimaginable and impossible exists and has its own reality and that it's important to share it with you to make of it what you will.

Another unimaginable incident occurred just after I had moved into my lovely lodge situated in a beautiful parkland forest. Before I bought it an old lady had owned it and died there. She had been a heavy smoker and often I smelt her cigarette smoke and heard her footsteps on the decking. My two cats and my dog often saw something moving in my sitting room when there was nothing there, but these are minor details. Being short of storage space I had a set of shelves installed in a cupboard by a very good carpenter who assured me that everything was secure and safe. Two evenings later there was a thunderous, explosive crash where the shelves had imploded and all my tins, dried food, crockery, glass vases were smashed and thrown to the ground. The carpenter said there was no way that could have happened as the wooden shelves were strong and could not have collapsed.

Again, I have no answers, no explanation how that could have happened, except that strange things do occur when a force from beyond steps in and for whatever reason it materialises objects and makes extraordinary things happen, proving that we are not the only ones inhabiting our planet and that there are 'things in heaven and on earth, that we couldn't possibly comprehend.' Objects appearing from nowhere through the ether descend and I am shocked, as there is no possible explanation for their appearance, for example a silver ring I bought many years ago when I was a young teacher in the shape of a musical treble clef, kept lodging into cupboard handles and doors and one time nearly took my finger off, so I threw it away in the bin. I was living at the time in a flat in North London. Many years later it mysteriously appeared one night when my son was staying with me in York, North Yorkshire. There was an explosive crash as pictures, ornaments and books were thrown to the floor from the upstairs landing. The ring appeared on the stairs and I was amazed to see it after having thrown it away many years previously. Somehow I misplaced it again and had forgotten about it until my Granddaughter, years later, saw something appear on my mantelpiece, shining in the sunlight. She pointed it out to me and I was shocked to see the musical ring again and felt it was a sign to wear it, so now it is on my finger but I now wear it upside down and it hasn't caused any problems.

Similarly, my eldest daughter had an engagement ring which she thought her ex-boyfriend had stolen, but one Saturday afternoon in my kitchen, I was cooking lunch and stepped backwards onto something small and hard. I turned to look and there was a beautiful, small diamond ring under my foot. It turned out to be the ring my daughter had lost six years previously. I cannot explain this phenomena as it is unexplainable.

How can you account for a mountain mysteriously appearing through thick mist in your back garden? When I visited my elderly Aunt Emily, who was a potter, on the Isle of Skye, she told me of a strange happening of when she and Uncle Gilly first moved to the old farmhouse. The ancient building had belonged to a legendary old woman called, Bella Marie, who was famed as a healer. The old cottage needed a tremendous amount of restoring and renovation, so there was a large crew of men working on the plot. Outside the kitchen door there was a large stone and little by little the stone began to change shape and develop human features. The men secretly noticed the transformation but kept it to themselves, until one day when the renovation was complete, the stone had metamorphosed into an exact replica of Bella Marie's face and Emily moved her indoors in the sitting room next to the fireplace where she could be part of the house again.

One morning, when I was staying with Aunt Emily and Uncle Gilly, I woke and looked out of the window to discover a deep mist shrouding everything in a steel-grey blanket of swirling vapour. The dense fog pressed into the window-panes, sealing out the landscape and drowning the cottage in a hazy, ghost-like sea. Emily and Gilly were at breakfast in the kitchen and seemed quietly subdued. Uncle Gilly joked about the fog but Auntie Emily hid her apprehension by busily making toast and spreading her home-made marmalade generously over each slice. We silently sat at the kitchen table as the fog peeped behind shadows like a hushed thief creeping under the doors and through the cracks in the windows. It is hard to describe the 'nothingness' as we sailed in a white limbo, like a lost ghost ship drifting on an empty sea.

Suddenly the sun broke through the veil and shone a bright beam onto the kitchen sink. We all heaved a great sigh of relief and Uncle Gilly opened the door and we stepped into the chilly garden. The fog was lifting inch by inch and I looked across the meadow as a massive mountain unveiled itself. "Look Uncle, you can see the mountain!" I declared feverishly, but he looked baffled and replied; "But there is no mountain here. There never has been!"

We were all unnerved by the appearance of the dark massive mountain towering into the sky and Uncle urged us to return indoors. Had we landed in a parallel universe or had another universe landed on our doorstep? We will never know. As the mist slowly dispersed, the mountain disappeared into the ether and all returned to normal. The meadows, the sheep grazing in the fields, the scurrying rabbits through the hedge, the birds singing in the trees, the babbling brook in the ditch all returned and we were left pondering the whole strange encounter but we never talked about it again.

Things that go 'bump in the night', unfathomable incidents, materialization of objects through the ether, close encounters of a third kind cannot be analysed and dissected like a rodent, etherised on a lab table to be labelled and scrutinised; for these mysteries remain forever enigmatic until such a time when we understand the profound craftsmanship which lies behind life's inexplicable tapestry.

GILBERT AND BUTTFACE

In Louisiana, not far from New Orleans is a big house, an Antebellum House, which was built in a particular style for plantation owners, where the Master of the cotton plantation used to live with his family. Slaves working in the fields lived in little wooden cabins on the edge of the cotton grasslands and oftentimes were cruelly treated and murdered. Their lives were spent enslaved to the Master, who owned them body and soul, until such time when the slaves were freed and the terrible era of malice and brutality ceased towards the yoked people.

The Antebellum House of which I speak, has been left in disrepair for many years and long gone are the slaves and days of heartless, merciless, vicious treatment of human beings by the white Masters. But I have a story to tell, a strange true story. You see when I was a little girl, my Pa bought the Antebellum House of which I speak and restored it to its former glory, not to bask in the fortune of the slave traders or take advantage of the slaves, but to celebrate the dignity and courage of the people who died there, because you see Pa was a kind, caring man and had known ill-treatment first hand as a young apprentice to a malicious land owner, but with hard labour had made his fortune honestly.

I was nine years old when he took Ma and me to look around the Antebellum House; we had no idea he was going to buy it! Pa drove us in his charabanc motor to a cotton plantation which was no longer part of the big house as the mansion itself, was being sold separately in a few acres of its own grounds and as we drove up to the palatial, black iron gates, the sun shone a golden pathway through a magnificent archway of ancient trees. The impressive building looked like a huge square box with four-sided arched balconies above and the same below. It was built in the Antebellum style of its era and must have been truly magnificent in its heyday.

A fine, business-like lady met us at the door and apologised for the house being neglected for a long time, but she explained that with dedication and money it could be beautifully restored. She had a very large, old-fashioned key to the open the door and as she did so, the cloudy memories of a past era cascaded upon us, shaking down dust particles from the fantastic chandelier catching the daylight sun after a long time hidden in the dark. Little shards of rainbow particles danced a merry pattern on the sad walls. A beautiful staircase wound up and around to bedrooms above and double, tall, ornate doors with golden handles lead to adventures beyond.

Pa said to go and explore while he and Ma talked to the nice lady. I ran into the sitting room ghosted by white sheets covering elegant furniture and there was a grand piano protected by a fringed, red blanket and huge mirrors dulled with time, trimmed with tarnished gold scrolls; it was like a forgotten palace. Carefully I pushed open a door into a dining room where a long, dusty table lay forlorn and the ornate silver candlesticks overhung with bits of beeswax stood tall and elegant waiting to be lit once more. Another door lead to the kitchen where a very old fella sat in a rocking chair by the ancient large stove

"Come in, come in Missy, don't be shy!" he said, smiling a toothless grin across his shiny, ebony face.

"Oh I'm sorry, the lady said there wasn't anyone here!"

"Well she be wrong then, 'weren't she?" he laughed, wrinkling his furrowed forehead, "come sit here" he said pulling up a little wooden stool next to him, "come on, say hello to old Buttface!"I hadn't seen the little ugly, pug dog sitting on his lap, nor noticed the gentle smoke curling from his grey, clay pipe.

"Come on then, tell us your name-mine's Gilbert, pleased to make your acquaintance!" He extended his gnarled, old hand to shake mine and I noticed strange markings engraved on his arm.

I said," I'm Arabella Watkins."

"That's a fine name, for a fine young Missy, now aint it?" He declared, sucking on his pipe.

"Do you live here? Pa said no one has lived here for a long time!"

"Well now he be wrong then?" stated Gilbert thoughtfully," but I weren't born here. Oh no! I was born in a slave cabin on another plantation not too far from here."

"You were a slave? You must be very old and sad?" I innocently remark.

"No, not sad Missy. Them days are over and we got to look to the future. You is right though, it was a bad, bad time and my Ma, God rest her soul, was one of them there slave girls working at the big house and the Master of the house, he take a fancy to her and well that's how I was brought into the world. He sent her to live in a little cabin on the edge of the plantation where folks couldn't see us. But I was marked as one of his." He testified pointing to the mark on his arm where he was branded. "The other kids around called me Cofi because I was black like black coffee with white cream and I neither belonged to my black brothers or any whites. I lived with my Ma for seven years and then I was brung to this house. A man with a horse and cart come to take me and he throws a little puppy pug dog at me saying," here take Buttface, you son of a ...! Well I thought that was the little fella's name and I called him Buttface from then on!"

I laughed at the thought of him being a little naïve boy, but sad he was dragged away from his Mother. "So what happened to you?" I questioned.

"Well the people here was kind, you know, probably on the count of the fact that I was the son of a Master. They gave me a little room of my own right at the top of the house in the attic with a real bed and for the first time, that first night, I slept in a real bed with little Buttface curled next to me and it was heaven because I had only ever known prickly straw to sleep on and the little biting insects that keep you awake at night which trample all over ya."

"Did you get to see your Mum again?" I asked earnestly, watching him blow smoke up the old charred chimney.

"Well Missy, no I did not, but I knowed she thought of me every day until her last breath."

I nodded, silently imagining the old lady but the silence was broken as Gilbert explained," I was brung here to be apprentice to the old butler. He was also called Gilbert and was going to train me as his apprentice because his old legs was getting too weak to climb all those stairs and run errands and serve food and wait on the family and I was given fine, fine clothes to wear just like big Gilbert. I was little Gilbert and became his shadow. I learnt the job real well Missy and by the time I was seventeen and old Gilbert had passed, I was a real fine butler. I done good for the family as they did for me."

"Ah that was lucky that you didn't have to labour in the fields like the other slaves."

"Yes Mam, I was real lucky, cos many of my brothers and sisters had to wear chains round their necks and ankles and that 'aint no fit way to live Missy, now is it?"

"No, certainly not, it must have been awful?" I added sympathetically.

"Well, I was lucky alright because I fell in love with a pretty little kitchen maid, my Rosebud was the cutest little thing you ever did see and we got married. I was eighteen and she was seventeen and the family gave us the gatekeeper's lodge to live in. Why me and my Rosebud we had a happy life together."

"Did you have children," I enquired.

"Well, no God did not provide us with a family but my Rosebud she was Nanny, the best Nanny in the world to the little children in this house and they loved her and she loved them with all her heart and soul and when they growed up and left, it darn broke her heart. But they visited from time to time and brought my Rosebud all kinds of gifts which she kept unused in her chest of drawers."

"Where is she now?"

"She's in heaven Missy."

"Oh I'm sorry!"

"Don't be sorry Missy, she's happy and resting 'til I join her and me and Buttface keep watch until it be right to leave."

Buttface grunts and shuffles on his knee and Gilbert pats him affectionately.

I hear Ma shout from the other side of the house and I hurriedly say good bye to Gilbert and run to see her, forgetting all about my meeting because we had lots to think about as Pa made the deal to buy the house.

The day we moved in was exciting and a great adventure. I was going to have my own room next to Ma and Pa's at the front of the house overlooking the great driveway. Ma was busy in the kitchen organising everything and she had a helper Mrs. Barton who was sorting through drawers discarding old cutlery when she found a very old photo and showed it to Ma who showed it to me.

"Oh that's Gilbert and Buttface!" I casually stated.

"How do you know Arabella?" asks Mum, a little concerned.

"I just know!" and I ran off to play as there was so much to explore.

Ma didn't ask again about Gilbert and Buttface and had the photo removed to an old desk in the attic. We never went there.

Now time has been and gone and the house isn't mine anymore. All special places have layers upon layers of memories embedded in the fabric of the walls and those energies live on and on side by side without clashing into each other.

I pass through the walls unseen by the new family but the little girl Emily knows me well and keeps me as her secret friend. I am following her and her Mum up the myriad of stairs to the attic where they are going to sort through old memorabilia. On the desk is the old photo of Gilbert and Buttface.

"Oh look here Emily at this old photo?" Urges Emily's Mother, holding up the old, sepia picture for her daughter to inspect who shrugs her shoulders nonchalantly, adding casually, "Oh that's Gilbert and Buttface! They're my friends!"

SHE'S WAITING IN THE SHADOWS

"She's waiting in the shadows!" A voice whispers in my dream. "She's waiting in the shadows!" The voice echoes the words until I open my eyes in the bleak darkness and wake. I repeat in the echoing stillness-"She's waiting in the shadows!" attempting to remember the dream to learn the meaning behind the message and a vision suddenly appears of a young girl dressed as a Nanny in the Victorian era. She is pushing an old-fashioned perambulator through the cemetery in the dead of night. She is waiting underneath a large cedar tree for a well-dressed young woman who is scurrying through the trees towards her; that is all I witness. I retrace the scene many times in my mind, but nothing more emerges. I cannot forget the words-"She's waiting in the shadows," which haunts and taunts me!

I am renting an old cottage for six months, situated next to a fourteenth century ancient church and halfway down the rickety stairs is a small, original window. The pane of glass is bubbled like a babbling brook and I wonder how many decades it has taken for the globules to form. I have read that scientists have discovered in the ancient city of York, that glass is actually a liquid! I can believe it, as the glass looks like it's dripping tiny droplets of liquid particles. I trace my fingers over the glass knolls and peer through them seeing beyond the antiquated, decrepit gravestones appearing in a bubbly sphere. It is especially eerie at night by the light of the moon when the white gravestone slabs gleam like stark ships, silently claiming that life is no more. It's odd to think that all those decaying bodies lying underground belonged to real, living people and that every person had a story to tell of their life here on this planet.

"She's waiting in the shadows!" The words circle in my head and I am intrigued to know who is waiting and why. I close my eyes to go back to the scene. Yes! I see the Nanny surreptitiously wheeling the perambulator over the bumpy grass waiting under the Cedar tree for the well-dressed young woman. I watch as she scurries over to the maid and peers into the pram. She seems overjoyed to hold the baby and the maid furtively glances around to spy any watchers. Her happiness is fleeting as the maid places the baby back into the pram and the young woman flees into the trees out of sight. The scene clouds and disappears.

It is twilight and I have lit a fire, toasting my toes in the warm glow, watching the amber flashes of flames rise and fall as the wind creeps down the chimney. I am a little tired and allow my eyes to close and without warning, I am hurled back into the strange scene. The maid is racing with the pram towards the tree, I hear her skirts swishing as she hurries and she is mumbling to herself..." oh please God, don't let us be caught?" The elegant young woman in a dark green jacket and hooped long skirt, briefly hugs the maid, saying,

"Thank you Mary, thank you. I must see my baby daughter. Is she well? Is she content?"

"Yes Madam, Violette, she is well and fine!" The maid hands the baby to her and for a few brief moments Mother and baby unite and milk for the newly born flows freely. "You must go Madam, it isn't safe, I said I would take the infant for a night stroll to settle her to sleep, but I am not sure the Master believes me. Quickly, you must go!"

Violette wipes away a stray tear and runs into the darkness.

I wake to find a few embers glimmering in the dark, but mostly ash remains-'ashes to ashes, dust to dust'. I rise and sleepily climb the stairs briefly glancing through the little window where a full silver moon is shining, gleaming a pathway over the grey headstones. The dead rest. The dead sleep, but part of their memories are alive. Part of their living resides with us forever locked in secret places, caught on the whistling wind, felt in dreams or seen in visions casting shadows in the dark.

A few days pass and I am busy with work and mundane routine with no time to ponder anything other than my own problems, but now, in the quiet Sunday evening timelessness of the Sabbath, the moon peeps through the trees snaking a shiny trail through the cemetery. I rise to sit on the stairs next to the little old window to gaze at the graveyard. Something gushes through the trees like a shiny spinning tornado and whirls past the Cedar tree, then disappears leaving no trace of turmoil in its wake, only solitary peace. I sit for a while contemplating the energy rush, remembering similar instances where I have seen ghostly vapours rising from the ether. Extensive research reveals that such energy pulses can sometimes be the result of a vibration emanating from a strong memory, albeit a good or bad imprint. Sometimes it is ectoplasm, which is a substance created by a lost spirit returning to earth's atmosphere and just as easily as it appears, it disappears. Scientists say that everything is a 'vibration' and as such can be manipulated and can be accessed by those who are able to tune into the frequency.

I go to bed but find sleep difficult as my mind is whirring with thoughts of mysterious visions and the whispered message in my dream-'She's waiting in the shadows'. I repeat the message in my mind and am taken back to the vision where Mary the Nanny takes the baby to her Mother Violette in secret to meet under the Cedar tree in the cemetery. I hear voices:

"Oh my lady! The Master is going abroad and will be taking baby Celestine and I am to go with them to look after her!"

Violette gasps and clenches her fists, cursing her husband, declaring she will not let him kidnap her daughter and will do everything in her power to prevent it. Just as she is lifting her outstretched arms to the cosmos to cement her promise, lightning spikes across the stars striking a large branch of the Cedar tree which crashes onto the ground in front of the women, just missing the sleeping babe lying in her pram. The two women are shaken and stand back, shocked by nature's raw power. The scene dissolves into the dark night.

I look at the clock. It is just past midnight- some say it is the 'witching hour' but I am sure that is superstition. As I creep down the stairs the moonlight catches the bubbly window and I stop to stare into the magical bubbles appearing like mini crystal balls. I stare into the largest glass dome and half close my eyes as in the ancient art of screeing. I hear distant voices arguing then see a man and woman screaming at each other. In untethered anger he lashes out and knocks her to the ground. She hits her head on a sharp rock and lies bleeding. The man, shocked by his action, gently picks up his wife, Violette, and is relieved she is breathing.

I pull back from the brutal scene and lose the vision. I try to go back into the crystal ball but the energy fails. I make a hot drink, shivering in the kitchen partly from the cold and partly from the shock of the vicious attack. The heat from the hot chocolate is warming and soothing helping me to calm my nerves and I decide to go back to bed. What is happening to me? Why am I seeing these visions? Why am I so involved? I think I am going mad. Perhaps it wasn't a good idea to leave my husband because of his affair and set off on my own living like a hermit in the lonely countryside. Perhaps I am not cut out for this 'aloneness'?

Monday morning and the round of work, eat sleep begins again for another week. Back in the hamster wheel of earning a living, I am too tired to think about strange happenings in the Churchyard, until the solace of Friday evening pushes me to wallow in self-pity but I refuse to feel sorry for myself and fight the greying depression sinking into an odd dream. I see Violette dressed in her wedding gown running through the cemetery towards the Cedar tree where she stops and leans against the soft bark. She tilts her head back gazing up at the stars and takes out a small purple vial quickly drinking the contents. She slowly drops to the ground. Time folds into a spiral, spinning like a Katherine wheel, exploding golden firefly flashes into the night as her dress fades and folds into the earth. Her flesh decays and her bones lie bare under the ground in an untimely grave. I wake from the dream and realize piece by piece Violette's story is unfolding and I question –why me?

Saturday morning and the grey rain is endless. A steel lid engulfs the village in a depressing mantle of sunless nothingness and I wonder what to do with my free morning. As I pass the little window on the stairs I see a bevy of middle-aged ladies parading into the church with mops, buckets, dusters and bunches of freshly cut flowers. I presume they are cleaning and decorating the church for Sunday service and a thought pops into my mind that I might go and talk to them to see if anyone knows the history of the Manor House, or the people from there who might be buried in the cemetery.

As I open the old, ancient creaky door, the smell of damp, stale cassocks and fresh lavender wax polish permeates the air. The clatter and chatter of busy women cease as I enter. Awkwardly I introduce myself and ask if anyone can give me information about the history of the Manor House and its occupants. The women natter amongst themselves, then one steps forwards saying," Oh are you the lady renting the cottage?" I nod and she continues," Well, it's Mrs. Kilmarnoch across the green you need to speak to; she keeps all the village records and knows all about our history, you should go and ask her- she'll know!"

I thank her and disappear making sure to close the heavy, ancient door, leaving the women to their sacred chores. Across the green is a lovely solid stone house flanked by laurel bushes and lilac trees. I am a little nervous about cold calling Mrs. KIlmarnoch, but I am prepared to take my chances, if possible, to learn about the mystery which is haunting me and I am relieved to find a very, friendly, warm-hearted lady who is only too willing to talk about her passion- village history!

Mrs. Kilmarnoch, a lonely widow, is overjoyed to see me and enthusiastic to share her vast knowledge over a hot cup of coffee and rich tea biscuits. I ask her about the Lord of the Manor and she raises her index finger proclaiming," Ah yes, let me see Lord Trevellis, the old Lord that is, was given land by the crown for his service to the kingdom and he built the Manor House. Lady Trevellis had a son and heir who became Lord Lucas Trevellis who married the Vicar's daughter, Violette. Now in those days my dear, a Vicar's daughter was considered a very lowly, commoner and certainly not good enough to marry a Lord, heaven knows, girls were second class citizens and had no rights of their own!"

I nod in agreement and think how far women have progressed and thank goodness for Emmeline Pankhurst fighting to gain the right for women to vote. Nowadays we take for granted women's role in society and our freedom to do and be whomever we please.

"Yes, my dear, you see, in that era, a woman's place was in the home, so men thought, and if you were not married or engaged by the age of eighteen you were considered a spinster; which meant social imprisonment for life and the sentence was to stay at home and become your aging parents' carer."

"I can't imagine that! It must have been dreadful?" I add taking a sip of coffee.

"I know, it seems quite preposterous now, but then a woman had only three choices available to escape home captivity and they were to become a nun and endure another kind of sentence, or to be a Nurse, which if you didn't have the stomach for it was another kind of confinement, or to be a teacher which perhaps wasn't as bad a choice as the others. But most of all marriage was considered the best option as you were nothing my dear, without the custodianship of a man!"

I hadn't thought about the life of women in that era as being quite so incarcerating but in truth, when examined, it was quite shocking in the light of today's opportunities.

"You see now dear, how shocking it must have been when young Lord Lucas Trevellis fell in love and married Violette? The trouble was that he was a totally spoilt, mad-headed young man, given to raging fits of temper and was completely indulged by his Mother and of course he could do no wrong in her eyes. When Violette had baby Celestine, who, the young Lord thought was another's child, he banned her from the house and took the child abroad with him. Violette, dressed in her wedding gown, poisoned herself and there is a modest gravestone in the Church, under the Cedar tree which Lord Lucas had erected on his return, having allowed her body to be buried, not in the main part of the cemetery, as the act of her suicide wasn't allowed by the Church, but in the quiet shade of the tree. On his return, he was a changed man after having learnt that his wife had not been unfaithful to him and that Celestine was their legitimate child. He had seen Violette meeting secretly with a man whom he had mistaken as her lover, when in fact she had agreed to secretly meet with her brother to help him with his gambling debts and to give him money to flee the country."

"Poor Violette, I feel so sorry for her!"

"Why do you say that so earnestly my dear, you sound almost as though you know her!"

"Well I ..."

"I know, don't tell me you've seen the visions?" Questions Mrs. Kilmarnoch, sympathetically.

I nod and wonder how she knows.

"Don't worry my dear, you are not the first and you won't be the last to be called to the grave in the shadows. It must be that somewhere along the line you are related to Violette. She always calls those who are part of her lineage, the girls, or women in the family, as she wants them to know her story and to be grateful for all that has been achieved and will be achieved in the future. Now that you know her story you must go to her grave and pay your respects. After that the visions will cease and you will move on but you will never forget that she is eternally 'waiting in the shadows to embrace all in her family fold."

'WHODUNNIT?'

Hidden in walls built of bricks and mortar, in houses, schools, hospitals and anywhere the living have resided, are memories, which are the fabric of life and like a heartbeat pulsing energy into being, they leave a residue, an eternal signature for those who can 'see', 'hear' and touch beyond the beyond. Even when buildings are destroyed, memories may remain locked and embedded into the vibration of the atmosphere. All energy, whether good or bad inhabit living substance, repeating its cyclical message, until the power wears out and becomes one with the universe quivering across stringed multi-verses. There are those who can tune into these memories, these vibrations, which haunt the places where powerful scenes of life, love, tragedy and disaster have been played out. Let me tell you story about an old lady…

An old lady sits in her wheelchair by a window gazing onto an old, cobbled courtyard, enclosed by a small wall, the remains of which, are the only bricks and mortar of a mansion house built in the eighteenth century but was demolished to build a modern care home for the infirm and elderly. The old lady stares intently at the wall. Her Carer breezes in enquiring," Adeline, what would you like to do today? It's a nice bright summer's day."

"I want to be outside in the courtyard by the wall. I want to see who did it!"

The Carer smiles and shakes her head accepting that Adeline's dementia and hallucinations are part of her condition. "Who did what Adeline?" She asks, straightening the old lady's bed.

"Why the murder of course, don't you know anything?" replies Adeline indignantly.

Her Granddaughter Lucy scurries in and kisses Adeline with great affection but the old lady does not recognise her. Lucy and the carer exchange sympathetic glances.

"She wants to go into the courtyard today to see her invisible friends!" Adds the Carer sarcastically. The women gently laugh behind the old lady's back.

"She's always been fascinated by history and solving past mysteries and such. I think she is interested in the history of this place, well that is the Mansion House which used to be here and she says that it was built by Sir Toby Barringer, who supposedly disappeared under strange circumstances." Affirms Lucy, affectionately wrapping a shawl around her Grandmother.

"Oh, I don't know anything about that! Now let's get her outside for a breath of fresh air!" States the Carer, unlocking the brake on the old lady's wheelchair.

"Is my daughter coming too?" asks Adeline holding out her hand to the young girl.

"Grandma, I'm your Granddaughter, don't you remember?"

"Is this young lady with you Beatrice? I don't have a Granddaughter, not that I can recall!"

Neither of the women reply but wheel the old lady into the old courtyard to sit by the ancient wall where it is peacefully quiet, except for the birds calling from a nearby tree. Lucy encourages her Grandmother to engage in simple conversation but the old lady is lost in her own world, so Lucy is content just to sit by her side for a while, understanding that it is only sometimes that her Grandmother recognises her. Suddenly the old lady opens her mouth and a strange male voice declares:

"Tis a fine house, a very fine house and will do me well, yes very well indeed!"

Lucy is shocked and looks around to discover the owner of the voice, but no one is around and the words definitely were spoken by her Grandmother.

"Grandma! Grandma! What on earth was that?" Lucy pleads shakily, frightened by the intrusion.

"You silly girl, why it's Sir Toby of course! See him over there."

Lucy glances at the old wall and sure enough a figure emerges from the bricks like a moving hologram. Sir Toby appears rotund, robust- a middle-aged man wearing a long black coat over a black waistcoat with a white shirt ruffled in a bow at the neck, with white tight trousers, like riding breeches and brown leather, knee- high boots. His red-hairy, long sideburns do not match his greying, brown hair. He is carrying a cane and a top hat in his hands, strutting around like a male turkey gobbler in charge of a roost of hens.

"Mrs. Danby, oh where is that damn woman? Mrs. Danby?"

Sure enough, floating through the bricks is his Housekeeper, Mrs. Danby. She is a stern, middle aged woman dressed in a black high-necked dress, black ankle boots with a black lace head-covering over her dyed black hair, which is swept in a tight bun at the nape of her neck. At her waist a bunch of keys dangle and jangle as she walks.

"I'm sorry Sir, I was busy with cook arranging your dinner tonight!" she affirms, politely curtsying.

"Ah, yes, well there's the rub you see, I will be dining out and everyone can take the evening off. Is that understood Mrs. Danby?"

"Why yes Sir, thank you Sir! May I enquire Sir as to where Sir will be dining?"

"No, you may not!" He sharply replies, agitated by her insolence.

She scurries out just as the Butler glides through the wall carrying a tray of drinks. Mr. Jack Hall is a well-trained Butler and knows his job and his place, having been in service for thirty years, working his way up from a boot boy.

"Your elevenses, Sir!" States the Butler, skilfully mixing a gin cocktail and placing the crystal glass carefully on a small reading table.

"Thank you Jack, but I've told you before- plentiful gin man, plentiful gin!"

Mr. Jack whispers to himself under his breath as he pours more gin into the glass," soon the cocktail will contain only a mere suspicion of Vermouth alla Vaniglia and be mostly gin! "

"What was that Jack?" interrupts Sir Toby.

"I said what a nice way to begin the day with plenty of gin. Hope this will be to Sir's liking?" Jack adds pointedly.

"No doubt, no doubt, it will be fine if you stop messing with it Jack!"

Jack bows awkwardly then slides back into the bricks.

"Wow, that's amazing Grandma, I've never seen anything so..."

"What?"

"So unreal but real! I think I am dreaming. Are you making it happen Grandma?"

"Oh, it's real alright! As real as real." She laughs, "but I have to find out something, do you see, I can't rest until I know?"

"Know what?" Ponders Lucy.

"Why who did it of course!"

"Who did what?" asks Lucy, puzzled and at a loss as to understand what she is experiencing.

"Oh for goodness sake girl, just watch and learn!""
Adeline points at the wall with her arthritic gnarled fingers as the Cook, Mrs. Blakely, crashes through the

wall in a petulant mood, shouting, "Well, it's alright for some! I've prepared his dinner and what's more the turkey tureen will go to waste, not to mention the guinea fowl and the lobster!" She wipes her red, care-worn face with a large white hanky and rubs her hands down her frilly white apron, ruffled over her grey, uniform dress. Her fading auburn hair is tussled beneath her white cap. "Something's afoot, I knows it. When the cream addles in the pot, it bodes no good mark my words." She sniffs and shuffles back through the bricks.

Beating a batter mix in a large bowl, Jemima, the maid, trips through the wall spilling some of the batter over her hands and face, eagerly enquiring, "Is it true? Is it true we can have the night off? That damn slave driver makes me work my fingers to the bone and no thanks do I get for it. Jemmy do this and Jemmy do that- is all I get morning, noon and night. Sometimes I just want to poison his bed time milk I do, just enough mind to make his life as uncomfortable as mine!" She accidently flicks batter in her face as she angrily points the spoon towards Sir Toby's portrait and trips back into the bricks just as Jacob, the young Footman marches through the wall adjusting his white bow-tie which he claims is always too tight and that his stiff uniform makes him twitch and scratch. He furtively looks around the room and tip toes towards Sir Toby's cigar box opening it carefully. In his white gloved hand he takes out a large Havana cigar and sniffs it and pretends to smoke it as the Master appears.

"Ah, Jacob there you are!" barks Sir Toby.

Jacob quickly replaces the cigar and pretends to polish the silver cigar box.

"My boots, my boots boy! I want to see my face in them like a mirror. Spit and polish, spit and polish and elbow grease my boy. All twelve pairs of them. See to it or you shall not be free tonight until they are shiny new!"

"Yes Sir, at once Sir, it shall be Sir as you wish!" Jacob bows subserviently, crestfallen as he doubts he can deal with twelve pairs of boots before teatime.

"Get to it, get to it then, don't dawdle boy!" Orders Sir Toby angrily, as they both disappear through the wall. An old man limps through the bricks wearing a grubby gardening apron over his shabby trousers with a red spotted neckerchief tied around his neck. He is carrying a small plant in a terracotta pot. He looks around the room and sighs and speaks to the Master's portrait. "Well Sir I did as you asks and plants a fine, fine bed of Geraniums and now you tells me I have to dig 'em all up as they makes thee sneeze. I dunno Sir, I works hard an nothing seems to please thee. I'm getting old an the work don't get no easier an the little you pay me Sir, don't cover needs, indeed not Sir, my Bertha says to ask you kindly for a little more!" He sadly bows his head at the portrait and limps back through the wall.

Mrs. Danby appears hurriedly through the wall, calling, "Bertie, Bertie? Has anyone seen the gardener?" Then she flips out of sight as the cook bounds in holding a small sultana cake. She glances around furtively, then steps back into the shadows and disappears as Jemima the maid trips in spilling a jug of milk and quickly attempts to wipe it up before she returns through the bricks just as Mr. Jack, the Butler marches in with the morning mail placed neatly on a silver tray and leaves the letters on his Master's desk and marches out again as Jacob, the footman enters wearing a hessian apron over his uniform with one black boot propped on the end of his hand but vanishes back into the bricks as Bertie the gardener limps in and straight out again like an actor making a mistaken entrance on stage.

"Whao!" announces Lucy in a daze, "this is all too much to take in Grandma. It's like all the characters are suddenly on speed and everything is gaining momentum. Please tell it to stop, I've had enough and besides it's getting chilly we'd better go in."

The old lady declines and wishes to learn more; it is as though she is commanding the performance and directing the play unfolding before them and instructs Lucy to stay put and witness the scene.

Sir Toby appears again, somewhat agitated and calls the household into his study stating officiously-

"As you all know, I am most grateful to you for your loyal service and it pains me to have to inform you that I will no longer require your services from the end of this month, as I am to marry Miss Montague Smythe and reside at her family's country estate."

A sigh of disbelief and dismay rises from the assembled household.

Sir Toby continues," This is most unfortunate for you all, but I have made arrangements for you each to receive a small sum as a token of my appreciation".

"But begging your pardon Sir, you said that as you have no heirs or direct family that on your demise you would leave the house to your staff to apportion it equally between everyone?" states the Butler greatly concerned.

"Indeed, indeed, I did indeed, but you see my circumstances have vastly changed and this arrangement can no longer be viable and in fact this very morning, Jacob, I wish you to deliver this letter to my solicitor making alternative provisions for you all. Now you may go and you have the evening to yourselves." Sir Toby dismisses everyone making sure that Jacob takes the important letter.

Through the wall the scene changes to the servant's dining room where everyone is assembled seated at the dining table.

"Well now! There's a turn up for the books!" States Mrs. Danby, "Who'd have thought the old miser would get engaged to be married, I reckon that is where he is dining tonight!"

"Miss Montague Smythe?" mimics Jemima in a posh accent, "well she aint no spring chicken and no looker either."

"I reckons they both deserve each other!" adds Jacob disdainfully.

"It's certainly not a match made in heaven that's for sure, but where does it leave us?" questions Jack.

"Up the bloomin' river without a paddle, I reckon!" states the gardener gruffly.

There is a moment's silence as they all ponder the situation as Jacob places the letter on the table for all to see.

"I guess that is the offending document Master Jacob?" inquires Mr. Jack the Butler.

"It is Sir," replies Jacob solemnly.

Everyone looks at it suspiciously and quietly moans.

"Yes, I must deliver it this very morning, post haste as Sir Toby wishes."

"Well what if it wasn't delivered?" questions Bertie, the gardener.

Everyone is shocked, shaking their heads, pondering the implication.

"Well, if it wasn't delivered then we'd still have our financial arrangement, wouldn't we?" states Jack thoughtfully.

"That's true enough!" adds Mrs. Danby.

"But Sir Toby would hear of it and write another letter," points out Jacob, knowledgeably.

"But what if there was no Sir Toby to …?" Jemima innocently utters as all assembled suddenly gasps at the idea and everyone shakes their heads in disapproval.

Alarmingly the upstairs drawing room bell rings making everyone nervously jump, as Mrs. Danby straightens her dress to attend to the call uttering,

"What does the old codger want now?" and she disappears through the wall leaving everyone to pretend to be busy with something.

"You see the plot, my dear? You see how things develop?" declares Adeline, totally immersed in the scene.

"Yes, Grandma it's very intriguing and enlightening of times gone by!" affirms Lucy, hooked on the story and both remain glued to the wall waiting for the next instalment.

The Carer watches from the bedroom window and is pleased that Adeline has company, not appreciating for one minute that the two are embroiled in a psionic experience.

Mrs. Danby returns to the servant's dining room in a vexed and agitated mood stamping her feet on the uneven flagstones declaring, "Why the old codger has changed his mind about this evening! He is still going out, but we are to stay and do extra chores!"

Everyone moans and Jack the Butler avows," if this aint the last straw! He deserves to be taught a lesson. Jacob where is that letter?"

Jacob hands it to him and everyone is shocked as he tears it into tiny pieces and throws the paper-like confetti into the air. At first everyone is dazed and then they all burst spontaneously into fits of giggles.

"Well, there we are then, we have no choice but to take action! What do you say everyone?" declares Jack. The staff are shocked and sit down quietly adjusting to the new situation.

"What does it mean?" asks Jemima unable to understand.

"I guess it means that we take the situation into our own hands and if there's no letter to deliver, we still have our original agreement in tact at the solicitors, which means…" Jacob pauses.

"We have to get rid of the old geezer!" affirms Bertie the Gardener.

Everyone agrees affirming the declaration like a jury pronouncing a verdict on the guilty party with the death penalty.

"But how?" enquires Jemima nervously biting her nails, and who…?"

"That's easy! It has to be all of us, or no one, understood?" affirms Jack, who is the senior mastermind behind the plot. Everyone agrees.

"Well, we all have an alibi because the old devil has taken away our free night and we all have to stay in and work, isn't that right everyone?" maintains Jacob, thoughtfully.

They all agree, except Mrs. Danby who is uncomfortable with the plot and asks, "That is all very well but how are we going to achieve our goal, so to speak?"

"That's easy too!" testifies Jack rubbing his hands gleefully.

"How?" asks everyone speaking at once!

"We all know that when the Master goes out on one of his evening soirees, he always comes back worse for wear and is quite frankly, drunk as a skunk!" testifies Jack, knowledgeably. Everyone agrees. "And we all know that he always takes the riverside walk home and on many occasion has been seen by onlookers to be dangerously too close to the water's edge. Is that not so?" Everyone agrees, "So I put it to you that we lay in wait until he perambulates precariously by the river on his way home and ....there you have it, no more Sir Toby!"

"Well I can vouch that there is a dangerous undercurrent in that part of the river because I fish there occasionally and everyone knows it's treacherous. Bodies are dragged under, never to be seen again!" adds Bertie.

"Who is going to undertake the dirty deed; we can't all push him in?" affirms Mrs. Danby.

"We all have to be there in hiding, because we are all part of the dastardly plot, otherwise it's no use," maintains Jack, firmly addressing the issue.

Everyone agrees." But who is going to do the- you know what?" whispers Jemima.

"It has to be someone young and athletic and nimble and bold!" states Jack, as everyone glances at Jacob automatically. Jacob stands up defiantly declaring, "I will do it if you are all behind me, so to speak, but on one condition, I get a little extra share of the agreement!" He smiles, proud of his wheeling and dealing skill just coming to the fore.

They all remain silent for a few moments before Bertie adds; "Well, I'm up for that then as the bounty will be sufficient to see out my days comfortably with Bertha. I'm not a greedy man, so long as all is fair!"

The ensemble listen and after a short consideration agree to the conditions set by Jacob.

"So it's agreed then we stay in and around the midnight hour when Sir Toby will be wending his weary way home, we will gather by the river and do the dirty deed", states Jack with grave authority. Everyone shakes hands and sets about their daily chores lost in thought.

"Oh dear, oh dear!" utters Lucy aghast at the scandalous scheme, but Adeline only nods and cautions Lucy to be quiet as the conspiracy is put into practice. They watch with bated breath as a scene unfolds in the darkness of midnight by the fast flowing river with only intermittent gas lights weaving a golden trail along the waterside.

A strange bunch of people gather under the bridge by the pathway that Sir Toby will take. They nervously whisper waiting for the lookout signal from Jack, who is stationed behind a tree waiting for Sir Toby to appear. Bertie is stationed by a bush near the muddiest part of the sideslip to act as a decoy when Jacob will run up behind Sir Toby and push him in the icy current.

Nervous tension builds as they wait, but it's not too long before they hear the drunken caterwauling of Sir Toby. "Oh will you, won't you, will you won't you, walk with me?" he sings tapping his golden cane on the walkway, slumping from side to side and hiccupping. Everyone is electrically charged with apprehension.

The scene seems to unfold in slow motion as Bertie, disguised as a beggar, makes a noise attracting Sir Toby's attention and from behind Jacob rushes at him, pushing with all his might as Sir Toby goes down with a thud on the ground hitting his head on a stone and is knocked out cold. A trail of blood trickles onto the muddy slabs. Jacob kicks the lifeless body into the gushing river and everyone appears from their hiding place to witness Sir Toby's face disappear slowly under the water. As the body is sucked beneath the grim reeds, they all scatter, disappearing into the night.

Adeline and Lucy gasp at the murder, shocked at the unbelievable treachery enacted by the staff and wait to witness the final scene.

Back in the Mansion House parlour all the staff are gathered to be questioned by a young detective who parades up and down by the fireplace asking questions. Jemima is crying behind her hanky; Mrs. Danby sits nervously twiddling her thumbs; Bertie stares aimlessly out of the window at his beloved Geranium patch; Jack is seated near the drinks table and keeps looking at his pocket watch while Jacob is loosening his tight collar.

"And you say you were all on duty on the night of Sir Toby's disappearance and were all here?" States Detective Superintendent Marcos formally addressing the group.

They all swear that everyone was in the house on that night. Mrs. Danby frowns at Jemima to stop her snivelling and Jacob scratches his neck nervously.

"It seems on all accounts that Sir Toby was somewhat inebriated after his evening's celebration and on his way back home by the river bank, slipped and fell into the river. There are scuffle tracks in the mud, apparently of more than one person in the vicinity at the time and traces of blood splattered on nearby stones, which could possibly indicate foul play," declares Mr. Marcos.

The staff uncomfortably respond to this information. Jack coughs, Mrs. Danby blows her nose, Jemima continues sobbing, Bertie takes a pinch of snuff and Jacob clears his throat. The Detective perceives this as a normal response from a dedicated and loyal staff feeling upset by the news. "Apparently his body was retrieved from the river this morning as it was spotted by a farmer drifting towards the lock." Jemima howls and Mrs. Danby quickly escorts her out through the wall.

"Well thank you all for your co-operation in this matter and I am sure the Coroner's verdict will be death by misadventure. I am sorry for your loss of a wonderful employer, whom I believe has made a very generous legacy for your loyal and trusty service. I bid you good day to you all." He slides into the wall leaving the staff quietly victorious.

Adeline sighs saying," there my dear, I now know the truth and can meet my maker peacefully." Lucy watches as her Grandmother slips away into another dimension somewhere in the great cosmos. Beatrice, the Carer strolls over to Adeline to wheel her in for lunch, but it is too late as the old lady has passed. Lucy hugs her Grandma and cannot explain what they have shared together that morning- it is a mystery and how do I know all this, because I am Lucy!

MIRROR, MIRROR ON THE WALL...

'Mirror, mirror on the wall, who is the fairest of them all?' Chants Janine as she admires herself in the mirror wearing a bright red wig and her Mother's blue floral frock. She jumps down from the chair to join her friends who are having fun dressing up.

"It's my turn to wear the red wig now!" whines Minnie, who is never satisfied and always wants what the others have.

"The green one is better for you," pipes up Gaina, "as it matches your Green skirt."

"I don't like the green one! It's my turn to wear the red one! Tell her Janine?" argues Minnie.

"Just look at this mess!" shouts Janine's Mother, entering the room abruptly;" and who said you could wear my frock Janine? Take it off at once and tidy up before your Dad gets back!" She slams the sitting room door and the girls scurry around picking up bits of material and clothes strewn over the floor and furniture.

"Your Mum's cross! I thought you said it was ok to use all this stuff for dressing up!" declares Gaina, bossily.

"Well, I thought Mum wouldn't mind if we just borrowed some of the costumes from her theatre box!"

"Well you thought wrong, and now you've got us all into trouble!" complains Gaina, "I'm going home!"

"So am I," affirms Minnie, copying Gaina as they hurry out the door leaving the mess for Janine to tidy up.

"Mirror, mirror on the wall, who do you think is the fairest of them all?" A voice from inside the mirror taunts.

Janine looks around puzzled by the voice and gazes up to the large mirror with the gold, guilded lilies carved around the edge.

"Yes, you!" echoes the voice, "You there! Who do you think is the fairest of them all?" it questions.

"I don't know! How should I know?" she retorts, upset that her friends have left her to tidy up and that she's in trouble with her Mum, and the voice is scaring her.

"What do you mean you don't know? You must know!" asserts the voice angrily.

Janine bursts into tears and howls," If you're so clever then you tell me!" The mirror is silent and Janine stops wailing. She scrapes a chair along the floor and places it next to the mirror and climbs up to peer into the glassy surface. Her reflection is normal and the room behind her reflected in the glass is the same as usual. There is nothing different. She presses her nose against the glass watching herself make a funny face. "That definitely isn't the fairest face of them all!" A voice from within the mirror chides and Janine almost falls backwards off the chair in shock.

"Ah ha! Caught you off balance! What can be swallowed, or can swallow a person?" the voice teases.

"I don't know, that's a stupid question!"

"It's not a question, it's a conundrum! A riddle silly and the answer is 'pride' of course- you can swallow pride, or pride can be your downfall, don't you see?"

"No!" declares Janine defiantly.

"You know the wicked witch thought she was the fairest of them all and tried to kill Snow White but in the end her pride was her downfall. Get it?"

Janine pauses to think about the statement and places her hand on the mirror subconsciously contemplating the Snow White story without realising that her hand has disappeared inside the mirror. Suddenly she sees her hand on the other side of the glass and sharply pulls it back, clinging to it tightly with her other hand.

"That was a surprise wasn't it? Bet you didn't think that could happen? Why don't you come inside? It's easy. Just step in. Come on, you know you want to?" the voice tempts, urging her to go inside the mirror.

"I can't! It's not possible. You're tricking me!" retorts Janine.

"It's no trick and don't you know anything is possible on the other side of your mind? Just tell yourself you can do it and you will. It's simple. But if you're a cowardy, cowardy custard forget it! I don't want to waste my time with you!" The voice cuts out abruptly leaving a strained lull.

Janine decides to climb down from the chair and walk away but the voice interrupts," Oh so you're gonna give up? Don't you want to know what's on the other side? Aren't you curious, just a little, teeny-weeny bit curious?"

The voice fades as Janine's Mother enters shouting;" I thought I told you to tidy up this mess? Your Dad will be here soon and you'll be in big trouble my girl and don't you touch my costumes ever again, do you hear?"

Janine hastily tidies the room and replaces the costume box back in its place in the cupboard. She fears her Mother's temper and doesn't wish to be locked in her room again or be sent to bed without supper. She can't help it if no one else can't see or hear the things she experiences. Her brother is always teasing her and laughs at all the things she says calling her a 'nutcase'. She can't explain why or how she can see through walls or know when things are going to happen before they occur. Her Mother bursts into the room again declaring, "And another thing, your friends are not welcome here anymore, so don't invite them. They make too much mess and too much noise, now go to your room!"

Janine sadly walks up the stairs accepting the rules. She wipes away a stray tear and falls on her bed dejectedly. She takes comfort in her story book and loves to read and as a page falls open on the Snow White story, the words' Mirror, mirror on the wall, who is the fairest of them all?' stares boldly at her from the top of the page. She sits up and looks at her dressing table mirror and sees a hand inside beckoning her. She climbs off the bed and stands by the mirror as the hand reaches out to touch her. She jumps back in surprise but recovers and takes a step forwards so that her body presses against the glass and she is pulled inside.

"Janine, Janine, open this door at once!" her Mother bangs on the door, demanding her daughter to unlock it. There is no reply. "Your Father is going to get the ladder, so you'd better open the door pretty quick my girl!" The Mother threatens, clenching her fists thumping the door aggressively.

The Father wearily retrieves his long ladder from the greenhouse and places it carefully up against Janine's window and climbs up. He stares through the window and bangs on the window pane to wake his sleeping daughter who has fallen asleep on her bed. She wakes to see her angry Father shouting at her to open the window and she hurriedly obeys. He orders her to unlock her door and she immediately runs to the door and tries to unlock it, but the key is stuck and won't move. Her Mother on the other side of the door doesn't understand and thinks that Janine is deliberately refusing to open the door. So she threatens her with further punishments, as her Father calls her younger brother to put his hand through the small top window to open the larger one, so that his small body can squeeze through to unlock the bedroom door. This he successfully achieves and has no trouble turning the stiff key to let in his Mother who is fuming with rage.

Janine tries desperately to explain but her Mother flings her to the floor screaming," that's it! You're grounded and no supper for you tonight my girl, and no tv and you'll stay in your room until I say you can come out!"

Janine feels isolated and alone. No one understands her. She desperately needs to escape and vows that when she is eighteen she will leave home and the only mode of escape will be through education. Her getaway card will be her entrance to college and for that she needs to focus on studying hard and passing all her exams-and so that's what I did. I, Janine Bancroft flew the nest never to live there again.

I expect you are wondering what transpired that day when I was pulled inside the looking glass-but all I can tell you is that it was a dream. Quite simply, I fell asleep and I can't remember what happened. You ask about the voice in the mirror, but I cannot explain it but let me tell you this-

I am attending my first ball, imagine me from a poor working class family living in a small farming village going to a posh ball in London in one of the most prestigious hotels in the city. I so want to make a good impression. My parents do not support me and the only money I have is my grant, which is hardly enough to live on, but I am too proud to ask for anything. I am too proud to appear at the ball in a second-hand ball gown and for the first time in my life I have a little money of my own. The 'Biba' store with Mary Quant designs is on Kensington High Street, just a short way from my college in Kensington Gardens and I buy the most glorious white Swiss lace blouse, with long black flowing culottes and purchase my first shiny black high-heel shoes. I make an appointment at an expensive hairdressers and have my long hair arranged fashionably in a chignon. When I am ready I stare at the finished creation in the mirror and say out loud to myself-'who is the fairest of them all?' and I suddenly see little Janine pressing her face against the sitting room mirror wearing her Mother's theatre costume complete with red wig. I smile to myself as I am proud to have weathered the worst up- hill struggle to gain entrance to college and finally escape the sad house.

My beau for the evening is a smart young man from the College of Estate Management and he calls for me in a taxi. As we arrive at the amazing venue we step across a red carpet and follow other young guests into a magnificent ballroom. We wait patiently at the top of a grand winding staircase as each couple descends graciously into the glittering ensemble below. Now it is our turn and I feel so important and beautiful and perhaps' the fairest of the all!' I take my first step forwards with my boyfriend and my stiletto heel catches in my long culottes and I fall in front of everyone, down, down, and in slow motion I roll and tumble down every step until I crash in a pool of spilt wine at the bottom of the long staircase. There is a horrible, deafening silence. As I rise and wipe myself down, all eyes are fixed on me and showing I am unharmed everyone returns to their drinks and chatter and my boyfriend ignores me and takes up with his best friend's sister.

I stand alone with my back to the wall, near a large mirror hiding my wet, stained bottom. I am so embarrassed and ashamed! I look in the mirror and hear the words-"now who is the fairest of them all?" I see a hand in the shiny glass-it isn't mine! It is wagging a finger at me, chiding-"Pride cometh before a fall!"

I DON'T BELIEVE IN GHOSTS!

"I don't believe in ghosts!" pronounces Leila confidently.

"Well my Mum says there are strange things that can happen but she believes that ghosts are like angels who come to help us!" States Stella, sitting on Millie's bedroom floor, quietly contemplating what angels might wear.

"I know they do exist because did you see, 'The Painted Face of a Clown', the film where the clown is the ghost of a clown who died in a tragic accident in the circus, well actually he was murdered by another clown and he haunts this other clown who killed him...? Testifies Francis excitedly.

"Yeh, but that's a film dummy!" Declares Leila knowledgeably.

Millie listens to her friends gathered in her bedroom and is uncomfortable with the conversation as she is very nervous about such subjects like ghosts and spooky things.

"That Clown film is an eighteen! When did you see it?" Questions Leila, liberally applying lipstick which Millie borrowed from her Mum. "Does this colour suit me?"

The girls pause for a moment and shake their heads in unison.

"I suppose there are good ghosts and bad ghosts?" adds Stella brushing her long hair with Millie's new brush.

"I think ghosts are only bad, well you never hear of good ghosts, now do you, I mean…?"Affirms Francis, hurriedly wiping off blusher applied too heavily on her cheeks as Millie's Mum opens the door.

"Time for tea Millie, sorry girls to break up the fun!"

"That's alright Mrs. Bradshaw, we were just going, see you tomorrow Millie and don't forget my music note book you borrowed or Mr. Henderson will kill me?" Declares Francis, surreptitiously sliding a packet of menthol cigarettes into her coat pocket which the gang hadn't had chance to smoke.

The girls noisily race down the stairs and bundle out through the front door giggling. Millie watches them from her window as they hurry down the road. In the strained quiet of her room, she assures herself that there is no such thing as 'ghosts' and looks inside her wardrobe and under her bed just to make sure that she is telling herself the truth and then goes downstairs to join the family tea.

"Come on Millie, time for bed!" urges Millie's Father looking at the clock on the mantelpiece. "It's nine o'clock don't you know?"

Millie begrudgingly goes upstairs, complaining that her elder brother is still playing games on his phone but her Mum points out that he is older and will be up later. She doesn't like being alone upstairs at night when everything seems so threatening in the dark. She hurries to her room and quickly turns on the light. She doesn't like shadows. She doesn't like shadows which stare and watch. She doesn't like shadows which move or appear from nowhere and quickly jumps into bed without cleaning her teeth to hide under the covers, stuffing her pillow inside her safe cave. Suddenly, footsteps tread stealthily across her carpet. Her heart thumps loudly inside her chest and the palms of her hands are moist as she tightly grips her pillow. The bedclothes are suddenly ripped back and with her eyes closed she screams like a strangled banshee.

"Scardy pants! Scardy pants!" Taunts her brother, laughing, teasing his younger sister as their Mum scurries through the door, declaring; "Now what's all this fuss about? Henry are you up to your tricks again? You know she's nervous at night time!"

Henry scoffs and bounds out the room muttering under his breath as his Mum attempts to reassure Millie that her brother is just being a silly boy and that it's only a game. She kisses her good night turning off the light, as she closes the door behind her.

Left in the dark, Millie's imagination takes hold. She thinks she sees a strange creature crawling out of her stuffed toy cupboard. She hides her face under the duvet and listens to the heavy silence. Her heart beats so fast, she thinks it will jump out of her chest and her mind falls into a paroxysm of ridiculous fears, especially when a timid tapping on the top of her duvet, just above her head, fills her with abject terror. She attempts to scream but her throat is paralysed and no sound escapes. A furry, fuzzy hand pulls back the duvet and a large round, black furry face smiles a welcoming grin, revealing a row of white jagged teeth, sharp like a hungry shark about to snap up its prey. Millie shuts her eyes tightly and holds her breath but the monster gently strokes her cheek with its fluffy, curly claws. Millie blinks and jerkily sits up to stare at the creature. Fear vanishes as he places a paw on her shoulder and introduces himself in a funny gruff voice;

"Hello, sorry to frighten you, I might look scary, but I'm really a softie, a large soft toy- see…" (He stands tall on her pillow and bows but falls forwards and Millie laughs at his clumsiness). "My name is Fuzzy Mc Mac. His large wide, friendly eyes gleam in the dark as he slips down from the bed and she notes that his long gangly fuzzy legs are too lengthy for his fat, rotund body and his red, black- spotted shorts are too big. All in all he is a comic character, especially when he does a little hip-hop dance and lands ungainly with his thin legs akimbo on her pink, carpeted floor.

"You are funny, Fuzzy!" laughs Millie," but why are you here?" she questions walking over to him to help him to his feet.

"Well, you are afraid of the dark Missy, and many things which are strange to you, but do you know the best way to combat fear is to directly confront it? Don't let it win. Don't give in. You see fear breeds fear. The more you are afraid of something, the more it has a hold over you and the minute, no the second, you challenge it- it loses its power; it shrinks and slinks away to find someone else to scare. You must show you are in control and when you do, that fear can never win again!"

"That's all very well, but I'm not brave enough to do that!" Millie sighs, disdainfully.

"Nonsense! Stick with me and you'll soon learn a thing or two. Now let me introduce you to Minky, the slinky mischievous black cat. Minky sidles out of the cupboard and stares at Millie with her head on one side in a comic, questioning fashion. "You see black cats are lucky. They are a sign and symbol of feline, feminine power. A black cat protects and brings the owner luck. Surely you know that if a black cat crosses your path you will have seven days good luck?"

Millie nods her head and stares at MInky, who slinks towards her and winds her black furry tail around her ankles. "Witches have black cats don't they? I don't like Witches!" Affirms Millie defiantly.

"There are good Witches and bad Witches of course, but Witches in general are not to be feared as they are mostly wise women who possess secret knowledge of healing and divination." Adds Fuzzy assuredly.

"Does Minky belong to a Witch?"

"No, she is a free spirit and here to help you overcome your fears!"

"How?" queries Millie.

"You'll see and now let me introduce you to Stan the Man Snake, in his psychedelic pink spotted skin, slithering secretly into unknown territory, going where no snake has gone before."

Stan Snake slithers forwards and Millie throws herself on her bed, terrified of snakes. Fuzzy laughs and Minky yowls with delight as Stan curls his warm, long body around Millie's right leg. "Don't be afraid of him, he is here to help you Millie. Now stroke his head, he won't bite!" Orders Fuzzy, a little impatiently.

Millie obeys and dares to stroke Stan's head. To her amazement his skin is not slimy or slithery but warm and friendly. Stan uncoils himself from her leg and slides up to her arms where Mille holds him gently and is thrilled to be hugging one of her pet fears- a live snake!

"See there's nothing to it!" Adds Fuzzy, happy to see Millie overcoming some of her fears. "And here we have Hector, Gecko, oh hecko, what a Gecko is Hector, little lizard on the wall, how is it that you never fall, whilst walking up and down and around, you never fall down to the ground?" Sings Fuzzy while Hector shoots out his long tongue approvingly.

"I don't like geckoes!" Scoffs Millie, placing Stan on her bed who coils himself into a bright pink circle.

"Of course you don't because you've never met one before or had one as a friend and ally! Say hello to him, he's very friendly and clever, in fact he wrote a poem about me. Go on Hecko, little Gecko, tell her the poem."

Hector hangs his head shyly and Fuzzy prompts him again. He proudly lifts his head high and with bulging yellow-green eyes looking in both directions at the same time, begins his little rhyme in a squeaky voice saying; "Fuzzy Wuzzy was a kind of bear, Fuzzy Wuzzy had kinda curly hair, So Fuzzy Wuzzy was Fuzzy wuzn't he?" Fuzzy raucously claps and applauds Hector. Millie isn't amused and begins to wonder if she is in a crazy dream, with zany, wild characters.

"There now you have met all the gang and we're here to calm your fears and teach you how to cope when you have no hope!" laughs Fuzzy. "Come on we're going to enter the tunnel of fears and when you conjure each gruesome monster lurking in your mind, we are by your side to help you conquer all. Here is Minky by your side to bring you luck; Stan the man Snake slides by your side to strike out at anything which might attack and Hector can jump anywhere to ward off any malicious strange creature.

Millie gingerly holds Fuzzy's hand as they walk into a revolving tunnel with all her new friends by her side. The black hole, like a star gate into the cosmos sucks them into a coiling, curling mass of multi-coloured energy and with new-found strength and confidence Millie walks through the' valley of the shadow of death and fears no evil'. As they all appear unscathed through the other side of the portal Millie stands tall and unafraid. She thanks her companions and they vow to appear whenever she is feeling uncertain, fearful or unsure.

"And now my dear, we must say goodbye, but we won't be too far away, but before we go we have a little show to perform for you, c'os that's what we do! You see you must remember that life is a Masquerade...so you must never be afraid. Cue song and dance routine..."

All the friends line up before Millie and sing a peculiar song, dancing and cavorting in the most hilarious manner crooning-

"Masquerade, where life is played,

Out on a stage for all to know-it's just for show

It masks the truth-it's purely spoof

It's a charade, Masquerade,

So never fear, or shed a tear,

It's not what you fear, it's a Masquerade!"

At the end of the song all the characters fade back into the toy cupboard and Millie falls asleep.

In the morning Millie's Mum gently wakes her. In her sleep she is singing a song...'Masquerade, where life is played...'

"Singing in your sleep now? That's a change from screaming! Come on Millie time to get up or you'll be late for school!"

Millie wakes refreshed from her peaceful sleep and wonders about her amazing dream and the toys that came to life to help her. In school she seems older, more mature and her friends comment on her new look, maybe it's her new hairstyle or her new shoes? The first lesson is English with Mr. Davies, who the gang consider to be the best teacher ever, as he always has new, interesting ideas and inspires them to think 'out of the box!' On his desk is a pile of new books which he hands out as the latest class reader, explaining that the short stories are based on the author's true experiences and are designed to make the reader question, discuss and debate unusual topics and share their own unusual experiences if they have any.

Millie looks forward to receiving the new book but when it is placed on her desk in front of her she gasps in disbelief. The class turn to stare at her and Mr. Davies asks if she is alright as she has turned very pale. Millie doesn't reply and gulps back her shock. On the cover of the new book 'Strange Shorts' are her new-found friends!

www.ingramcontent.com/pod-product-compliance
Lightning Source LLC
Chambersburg PA
CBHW070446170726

48291CB00005B/1619